The Eridanos Library 3

Alberto Savinio

Childhood of Nivasio Dolcemare

Translated by Richard Pevear and with an introduction by Dore Ashton

Eridanos Press

Original Italian title *Infanzia di Nivasio Dolcemare*

First published in Italy by Einaudi Editore, Torino 1941

Distributed in the U.S.A. by Rizzoli International
Publications, Inc., 597 Fifth Avenue, New York, NY 10017

Cloth: ISBN 0-9414-19-04-5
Paper: ISBN 0-9414-19-05-3
LC 87-83300

Printed in Italy

Contents

Introduction

by Dore Ashton

Most commentaries on the work of Alberto Savinio sooner or later invoke the name of André Breton who, in the hyperbolic tone appropriate to his subject, paid Savinio and his brother Giorgio de Chirico the ultimate compliment in his 1939 *Anthologie de L'Humour Noir*: Their works, he wrote, were at the very origin of the entire modern myth. The brothers, who in their adolescence had referred to themselves as the Dioscuri, no doubt impressed the surrealist guru with their unflagging energy; their agile maneuvers to transform themselves into poets, musicians, novelists, stage designers, painters, and even, in their black way, philosophers. Despite his eventual disenchantment (he had, together with Aragon, written off de Chirico in a photomontage epitaph already in the mid-1920s) and despite the fact that in his anthology he had cagily noted that the brothers' work as progenitors of the modern myth had reached its culminating point on the eve of the 1914 war, Breton acknowledged the authentic qualities in the oeuvre and above all, the high quality of Savinio's writing.

Breton was in a good position to see Savinio's

strengths. He himself had experimented with concrete images as complements, or even more, as completions, of the written thought in his extraordinary novel of 1928, *Nadja*. Savinio's strong visual endowment was apparent to Breton who could fully comprehend Savinio's declaration in 1914, which Breton cites, that "far from those periods when abstraction reigned, our epoch will bring forth material itself (things) with their metaphysical elements complete. The metaphysical idea will pass from the state of abstraction to that of the senses." The gravity of these thoughts recorded in 1914 is juxtaposed in a proper surrealist way with one of Savinio's more riotous short stories in which his capacity for black humor is demonstrated to be superlative.

Savinio, that versatile magpie who called himself "a collector of experiences" in his preface to Nivasio Dolcemare, had issued works of literary merit all through his life in a kind of gyre in which he turned and turned, picking up all kinds of eclectic references like a great vacuum cleaner. (The image of the vacuum cleaner, I realize, I have found in Savinio himself who wrote in *Capitano Ulisse*, 1924, of "the set, the air of the theater, his immersion in the lofty atmosphere of the stage, his passage through this sterilizing machine, this superior *vacuum cleaner*.") The eclecticism marking Savinio's writings becomes the premise of the modern myth which Breton defined. Savinio defended his approach again and again in his writings, regarding eclecticism as a means beyond the commonplace materialism of most literature. But not only literature: As a composer Savinio would write of its value to music, and to all the arts, for that matter. Around the time he was writing Nivasio Dolcemare, Savinio wrote a commentary on Stravinsky in which he defended—

without, for once, irony—the necessity of mannerism in modern culture, and above all, the value of the paraphrase:

> Stravinsky is not a creator. His qualities lie in the paraphrase, the interpretation, the imitation. Each of his musical compositions is a "seen from". . . . The paraphrase of Stravinsky is less an evil of the epoch than a necessity of the epoch. It is found equally in Picasso, who now paraphrases the drawings of Ingres, now Pompeian painting, now African sculpture. (*Apollo musagete* in "Oggi," April 19, 1941.)

The writings of Savinio himself might be similarly cast as paraphrases. But having said that, we have only said that like Picasso, he had a generous appetite for varied experience which he incorporated, like bits of collage, into his ongoing prose poem. Not only does Savinio have a distinct flair for the condensed image, shaped inimitably in words, but he also has his own peculiar gait. His saunter through many climates—that he calls a novel—is consciously paced in an idiosyncratic way.

Savinio was destined to be something of a prose poet—at least part of the time—by the circumstances of his formation. The heritage that he so sedulously sequestered for easy access includes the early peregrination of the Dioscuri (who in the original myth, it will be remembered, were destined to spend alternate days in the upper and lower worlds) from Greece to Germany, where both brothers were well nourished on German romantic poetry. Savinio, three years younger, arrived in Munich in time to study music with Max Reger (at least for a while: Reger was called to Leipzig the year the Chirico family arrived in 1907). Whatever the duration of Savinio's exposure to Reger, the German composer left his impress. Reger had only recently declared that he was, in effect, creating "musical prose" in which musical elements could be released from symmetrical organization. In one of his works, *Schlichte Weisen*, Reger had attained what H. H. Stuckenschmidt* called "a collage-like effect" by almost eliminating bar patterns. This lesson was not lost on Savinio.

In addition to a musical education, Savinio acquired a liberal education in German culture. He and his brother steeped themselves in Nietzsche, one of the greatest of prose poets, whose influence was evident in the works of both brothers. Seven years later, Savinio would sign the score for *Niobé* "Alberto Savinio artisan dionysiaque" and in his 1918 *Hermaphrodito* twice refers to Nietzsche's idea of "the transvaluation of values." Still later, in Nivasio Dolcemare, Savinio reasserts Nietzschean principles. He says of Nivasio: "Destiny predisposed him to overcome the defects of his family, his caste, his race." This *Übermenschlich* vision is further extended when Savinio describes the hidden "superior" man in Nivasio, saying, "the superior man speaks a colorless, transparent, blank language." This man—Nivasio—when he did his army service was of course underrated: "No one ever understood that Private Dolcemare was *ready for anything*." In another passage Savinio describes Nivasio as a victim of democracy—a theme both Chirico brothers were fond of, and which derives directly from Nietzsche. (It is also possible that Savinio remembered *M. Teste* who also

**Twentieth Century Music,* London, 1969.

vaunted his normality, his colorlessness, and his being ready for anything.)

The brothers' sojourn in Munich yielded still more: both enlisted themselves enthusiastically in the ranks of the defenders of the mystical painter, Arnold Boecklin, who had died in 1901, and who was being argued over passionately when the Chiricos arrived in Germany. They were also keenly interested in the work of the painter and graphic artist Max Klinger who, largely thanks to the brothers Chirico, would have a curious impact on the art and literature of the 20th century. It was the Dioscuri who revived Klinger's strange fable, the graphic account of 1881 called (significantly!) "Paraphrase on the Finding of a Glove." De Chirico in his paintings, and Savinio in his writings, would reanimate Klinger's inspired tale, and it was probably they who alerted Breton and the other surrealists to the malleable and suggestive properties in the motif of the glove. Breton had made much of it in his novel-with-pictures, *Nadja,* where in at least three passages and one illustration the glove becomes protagonist. The glove as fetish or simile is notable in Chirico's paintings and turns up several times in Nivasio Dolcemare: In the early part of the book, the father sinks into sleep and "his enormous hand, palm up, creased with a capital M, lay on the floor like a glove." Later, Savinio moves closer to the insignia-like quality of the large red glove in Chirico's painting: "An enormous Red Hand hung at the end of Stadium Street, wrist up and fingers pointing to the sidewalk." Savinio being Savinio and not Breton, or even Chirico, takes the glove insignia into the realm of the mythic with tongue in cheek: The red glove, he tells us, is the sign of three sisters who are glovers, but whom everyone knows were really three sirens in disguise. "Informed sources said that the sign of the Red Hand itself concealed an immodest symbol; but who puts much faith in the language of symbols?"

Who indeed! Savinio himself saw poetic symbols everywhere. Both brothers battened on the Munich idea of the *Kunstlerpoet,* a category in which Klinger and Boecklin were principals. The heavy fragrance of German things would continue to linger in the armoire of Savinio's imagination, both in his painting and writing, but would be considerably adulterated by the images and traditions quickly appropriated in Paris in 1910. Somewhere along the line—it would be hard to say how and where—the brothers had decided to eschew the notion of originality. The firm denial of the importance of originality, expressed so emphatically and so often in Savinio's writings, enabled him, in a paradoxical way, to take in the most original of all phenomena in the seething cultural life of Paris. Basically Savinio believed, as he wrote in 1918 in *Valori Plastici,* that what he had to search for was "a state of intelligence, not an extravagant appearance of originality." Chirico, in his novel *Hebdomeros* of 1929, wrote of "the color of primordial inspiration, primordial and not original; Hebdomeros distrusted originality as much as fantasy." Since Savinio was absolved from seeking the grail of originality, he was able to undertake a sort of bee's flight that took him into various milieux in the Parisian avant-garde. He saw and heard everything and scavenged in many traditions. Even the slightest of his stories was redolent with allusions, sometimes from direct observations, sometimes from pilfered ones, and sometimes made up, like baroque riddles, from both. For Savinio, everything was *à clef.* Filippo de Pisis recalled his encounter with the brothers in Ferrara in 1915, remarking that both were writing "very evocative texts lightly influenced by Apollinaire and Cocteau." The natural ebullience of these two poets had attracted Savinio especially, and his life in Paris was considerably tempered by his deep admiration for Apollinaire. Certainly Apollinaire's youthful sojourn in Germany and his own foreignness provided an initial common ground. By the time Savinio arrived, in February, 1910, Apollinaire was one of the most successful avant-garde figures anywhere, writing poetry, criticism, newspaper gossip and pornography, as well as maintaining what was in effect his own salon. Soon after Savinio's arrival, Apollinaire became editor of an uncommonly interesting literary journal, *Les Soirées de Paris,* whose headquarters became a hangout for some of the liveliest minds in Paris. Savinio would later describe Apollinaire's small editorial office full of mirrors, designed to suggest "infinite space" and to set Savinio's imagination wandering. Nivasio, he would write, was one "whose whole life has been spent in a world of mirrors."

Savinio savored Apollinaire's irreverence and his high-spirited approach to tradition, at once full of healthy curiosity and respect, and capable of selective derision. Undoubtedly Savinio followed the older poet to his sources—Baudelaire, then Rimbaud, and of course, Jarry. Probably also he shared the excitement of the event of the year 1911 when Raymond Roussel's dramatic version of *Impressions of Africa* was performed to a choice audience of artistic rebels. Roussel's remarkable manipulation of language and his addiction to the pun, Savinio's own favorite word category—in Nivasio he speaks of the pun's "sacred character"—would have electrified the young writer. In fact, Roussel's fantasy language in *Impressions of Africa,* published in 1910, the year Savinio arrived in Paris, is notable for its colorlessness, a quality Savinio extols in

Nivasio. Roussel tells the most bizarre tales in a simple descriptive language paced in the flat-footed prose of a police reporter:

> On my left, with its back to a row of sycamores, and facing the red theater, stood a stone-colored building, which looked like a model in miniature of the Paris Bourse. Between this building and the north-west angle of the esplanade stood a row of life-sized statues. . . .

Roussel's statues, like many of Savinio's, could reasonably be called proto-surrealist. One was composed of innumerable corset whalebones, and another was on wheels with lines that "gave an accurate impression of a railway line." Roussel's fantasy is kaleidoscopic with one improbable scene sliding into another, with numerous secondary anecdotes and characters such as the Czar, Handel, and Prince Savellini, "an incorrigible kleptomaniac who despite his immense fortune, frequented railway stations."

Savinio was soaking up the *Stimmung* (a much favored word; Apollinaire would soon write of Professor Doctor Stimmung in *Le Poète Assassiné*) of this exuberant Paris, storing its phrases and verses in his acute ear and, at the same time, inventing himself as a composer. Apollinaire, clearly fond of his young acolyte, took considerable space in his May 24, 1914, column of *Paris-Journal* to describe a musical performance that he himself had arranged in the premises of *Les Soirées de Paris*. The text tells a great deal not only about Savinio as a very young man, but Savinio as an aspirant to the pantheon of avant-gardia, and his covert intention to become perhaps not original, but *an* original, as the French say. Apollinaire describes his young friend in shirtsleeves, a monocle in his eye, "screaming and throwing himself about while his instrument struggles to attain his own pitch of enthusiasm," a pitch, Apollinaire explains, that the musician maintains until his fingers are bloodied. This maniacal performance, oddly enough, is meant to reflect the "powerful severity totally in keeping with the austerity that marks our time." Here, Apollinaire probably is quoting Savinio who in his wildest and sometimes funniest sallies is always talking about the "austerity" of his style. Apollinaire had already offered Savinio space in his own magazine, and, in the newspaper article, quotes and paraphrases Savinio's views. "He believes that he can represent on the stage, and express in his music, all the strange and enigmatic aspects of life in our time; he also wants to make his music resound with the shock of the unexpected, of the truly singular." (Not a mention here of the doings of the Futurists that one can't help suspecting had a certain effect on Savinio, not only as a composer, but as a writer of words somewhat in liberty.)

Savinio was barely twenty when he first plunged into the Paris maelstrom. He was uncommonly receptive. No doubt he believed in that awkward idea, the Zeitgeist. From the rebellious and often satirical spirits of such figures as Max Jacob, Picasso, Cocteau, Salmon, Cendrars and above all Apollinaire, Savinio learned to defend himself from the inroads of French Cartesianism. Primitive things, primitive art, primitive passion were *en vogue* and Savinio was quick to see the logic of it. His great campaign, in his more serious moments (if there were any) was to rouse his readers from the mechanical torpor of reasoning. "Thinking," he would declare in a preface published in 1941, "is a synecdoche." (*Casa "La Vita"*)

It was from profound conviction as well as a temperamental tic that Savinio sought in his round of writings to bestir the other part of the human imagination, the part that could not think in linear terms but only in the great image-laden circuit of mythology. He primed himself with his memories of his childhood in ancient Greece. Despite his contempt for the decadent Balkan society he so successfully denigrates in Nivasio Dolcemare, his love of Greece, moored in the old pagan myths, is a central motif of his work. This childhood, so remarkably evoked in Nivasio, despite the richness of his Paris days, is the principal source of his imagery. He remains, as he says again and again in his writings and even his drawings and paintings, a Mediterranean man. In his earliest writings he announces it in the exalted tone of the Nietzschean: "From this ferment will spring the prototype of the Mediterranean genius—the man in the wings, the religious man, the man-pelican who rends his breast from whence gushes lightning and shade and a flaming heart!" (*La Voce,* February, 1916) Later, in *Hermaphrodito,* he called the Mediterranean "the sea of my destiny." Not for nothing is the pun Dolcemare, sweet sea and also bittersweet; and the choice and often beautiful language he invokes to describe his sea, as in Nivasio: "A youthful breeze ruffled the white clouds, curled back the locks of the Aegean."

Savinio is only half ironic when he peoples the world of Nivasio with the ancient Mediterranean deities, and describes his own father as having "a bearded centaur's head." His claim to the legacy of the pagan gods, far from being diluted by the strong currents in Paris, was only reinforced. Rimbaud, after all, had visited them too. Nivasio, as Savinio pointedly remarks, before entering life as a disguised ghost, "had spent a season in hell." Savinio had sought the solace of the Greek gods, as had his hero Nietzsche, but had found, as he says in Nivasio, only a "motheaten and weary" one. Still:

> The Greek God is less an Abstract Entity than a Demiurge, that is, a Working God, a Passionate God, a God subject to hunger, anger, cold and to the sky-blue happiness inspired by children's games; a God who leaves deep footprints behind him when he walks; a God who, wherever he rests his hand, leaves an imprint in the form of a fig leaf; a God who, when he breathes, warms the air and revives the greenery.

For all that, Savinio is a modern man condemned to the voice of irony. No sooner does he fetch up the gods than he bursts out with torrents of laughter. His humor, as Breton understood, was as serious in its blackness as the "austere" (to use one of Savinio's own favored words) thoughts of the humorless. Burlesque was Savinio's forte.

It is found everywhere in his writing and even his painting. In the verbal arts, Savinio distinguishes himself with irrepressible wordplay at various levels. He puns and travesties profusely. Above all he loves to play, in his anagrammatic way, on names, as Jarry and Apollinaire had done before him. Savinio becomes Nivasio and Nivasio becomes Visanio, and god knows how many other anagrammatic references there are. Sometimes names are not rearranged but are descriptive, as in the case of Dr. Naso, or the restaurant keeper Signor Stomachos, or the fat procuress with the turnip hands, Basilica. Often Savinio cannot resist the schoolboy urge to become salacious: In the comic scene in which various sergeants in the Greek army enjoy the favors of one of the many disastrous maids in the household, Savinio speaks of Sergeant Zizimakis and Sergeant Cosmazizis, relying on his French readers to recognize the slang word *zizi*, which can be roughly translated as prick. These wordplays, and countless scenes in Nivasio Dolcemare are downright funny. They ought not to be freighted with theoretical literary discussion. Nivasio, after all, deplores "the unbearable tendency of 'serious people' to dramatize the most trivial themes."

Savinio's play on names, extended to antonomasia, often moves into a play on images, those concrete "things" which Breton cites. An example is his description of the Lady of Ladies: "Bunches of fat grapes hung from her towering coiffure, and wood grouse fluttered in it." There are also sly combinations of the mythic and comic, as when, in order to get across his point about the decadence of Europe, Savinio describes a certain titled man seen by Nivasio with a pair of tall branching horns rising from his forehead "which transformed the baron into a living hatrack." The tottering Europe Nivasio so deplores lives in these ridiculous members of society, even those "born," among them the blind marquise whose son plays Antigone to her Oedipus.

The Dioscuri more or less part company when it comes to surrealist poetics. De Chirico's contempt for his erstwhile surrealist associates was never shared by Savinio, although he obviously preferred the softened version of Cocteau to the more abrasive exercises of Breton. On several occasions Savinio drew a distinction between his own works and those of the orthodox surrealist. He thought that surrealism was the expression of the unconscious, or that which consciousness "had not yet organized," while his own work does not represent the informal or express the unconscious, but rather, gives form to the unformed and consciousness to the unconscious. He defined surrealism in 1940, in *Prospettive,* as "the internal terror of man, his forests, his tempests, his dawns, his splendor . . . just as romanticism is: the terror of nature, its forests, its tempests, its dawns, its splendors." His affinities with the surrealists were never denied. In his 1945 preface to *Tutta la Vita* he speaks of couches, divans, armoires and other pieces of furniture as species of living, speaking personages that he had used in his stories, tacitly accepting the surrealist emphasis on the object with its expressive aura.

Savinio had contributed to the surrealist ethos. If Breton and his companions were enchanted by their encounter with de Chirico's mannequins, and the whole notion of metaphysical painting, it was, Savinio would claim, largely due to his own work. Recalling his designs in the first Italian edition of his *Chansons de la Mi-Mort,* he pointed out that the maquettes of the personages in his drama—The Bald Man and the Young Man—were the origin of the mannequins of metaphysical painting. From that moment on, the mannequin became a familiar prop in surrealist writings and paintings. In Nivasio Dolcemare, Savinio makes a small digression to denounce Cézanne, but does admit that Cézanne deserves the credit for leaving the faces in his portraits as "a neutral oval to which the viewer can imaginatively attach the face of a friend, a relative, a lady of his dreams or whomever he likes." Savinio's play with the mask or the blank face is usually couched in terms of burlesque as in the hilarious scene in the employment agency where the curtain opens and "Ten masks, ten mannequins, ten shooting gallery figures" are revealed soon to be followed by "ten sexless creatures who reproduce by authogenesis like single-celled molluscs." In the episode in the employment agency, the Fellini-like excess is at once funny and unnerving, but perhaps owes more to the *Tales of Hoffmann* than to the obscure depths of the Freudian psyche.

Savinio, that willful chameleon masquerading as a Demiurge (he quotes Tasso in the notes: "Either God inspires him or man makes a God of his own will") was obviously affected by his concourse with Eros as interpreted by the orthodox surrealists. The erotic episodes in Nivasio Dolcemare cleave quite faithfully to Freudian doctrine. Take for instance his allusion to fetishism: "Many years later, having read the Epistles of St. Paul, Nivasio understood that a woman's foot is a great instrument of lust, one of the most insidious weapons the Adversary can use to lead us into temptation." On the other hand, Savinio's rapturous wonder at the effect of the close-up, built in a series of "takes" much as if he were filming, is so compelling that the surrealist component seems negligible. He offers a moving and not at all ironic description of adolescent eroticism. He is never clinical. On the contrary, there are rare moments when he is simply tender, as:

> When Nivasio came back to his senses, his body was lying on the ground, his head resting on Cleopatra's knee, his face very close to the bare, wet feet of the island girl which because of the short distance, seemed huge, inhuman, monstrous.
>
> The passage from a state of unconsciousness to one of consciousness went almost unnoticed. Though awake, Nivasio was hypnotized by those

> two bare feet, which loomed before him like mountains.
>
> The sun irradiated the room. Invisible elements of air penetrated Nivasio's organism. . .

Even Savinio's similes in this chapter are more tender than the orthodox surrealist might allow: "The breast shone amid the lace of the blouse like a candied fruit in a perforated paper wrapper." Savinio is offering a slightly disguised *Bildungsroman* in Nivasio Dolcemare. The passages concerned with sexuality, including the horrifying voyeur sequences, are carefully sown throughout the tale. Irony is abandoned, then. With considerable novelistic skill, Savinio trails his eroticism like smoke through this collage of narratives creating a *Stimmung* saturated with eroticism. For instance, whenever girls or women appear in more desirable form, he enhances their erotic allure by enfolding them in the heat, the languor of mid-summer days in Greece. That Greece is meticulously characterized in some very well written descriptions of flora, fauna, and large vistas. The differing landscapes and climates of Savinio's childhood lend this novel a reality that cannot be called a surreality. Despite his apologia for lack of originality, and despite his occasional and deliberate thieving ways, Savinio was, as Apollinaire recognized, a devotee of "the truly singular" and contrived with his pen to present it.

Translator's Note

This translation of *Infanzia di Nivasio Dolcemare* was made from the edition published by Einaudi in 1973. My aim as translator has been to serve the original as faithfully as possible, in which I have been greatly helped by the clarities of Savinio's prose. I have even left in place two or three errors in the original, since with Savinio it is hard to tell error from intention. Two instances of my own ignorance have also been let stand. In the section entitled "Without Women," Savinio describes the inflections of Signora Perdoux's voice as tracing *una sonora fila di piccole montagne russe*—"a sonorous line of little Russian mountains." Why "Russian" mountains? I did not know that the Italian, and also the French, name for the children's playground slide with several ups and downs is "Russian mountains." (Incidentally, the Russians call this kind of slide "American mountains.") In the other instance, Savinio refers to the driver of the first motor car in Athens as a *riscaldatore*, a "warmer" or "heater." I could not see why a driver should be called a "heater," nor could anyone I consulted. Only recently did the obvious answer occur to me. The *Infanzia* was first published in 1941. Several years earlier, by his own account, Savinio had suggested the forming of a society whose members would pledge to remain unaware of Mussolini's existence and never to speak his name, "for hygienic reasons." One way Savinio used to make fun of the party in power was by following its nationalist language program to the letter, replacing even the most commonly used foreign terms with Italian versions of them. *Riscaldatore,* then, is simply a translation into Italian of the universal term for a professional driver—*chauffeur.* I mention these lapses here because I could not correct them in my version without explanatory notes, which would be contrary to the spirit of the text. Savinio has supplied his own notes, and I have preferred not to add to them.

R.P.

Preface to the Life of a “Born” Man

Nivasio Dolcemare spent his childhood and part of his adolescence in a Balkan capital, in the midst of a cosmopolitan society to which Europe sent its most exquisite representatives. The soloists of the Concert of Europe, the best names from the Almanach of Gotha, the brightest stars of the diplomatic caste were known to Nivasio Dolcemare, one might almost say, by smell. If the mythology of our time has so little hold on him, if it lacks charm and mystery in his eyes, it is because for the most impressionable, the most receptive part of his life, he lived at the very heart of that mythology. Was that good or bad? "Bad," Nivasio Dolcemare thought for a long time. And during his youth, with the Don Quixotisms that accompanied it, Nivasio combined a stinging contempt for the upper classes with a trusting if somewhat mannered sympathy for the frank, simple, untouched virtues of the people. This society was composed of the local aristocracy, the court, select members of the various European "colonies," and the entire diplomatic corps. There could have been no more favorable place for learning the feel of that limp, drawing-room Europe, that Europe of "good Europeans,'' which threw up its already weak and debilitated hands with the first cannon shots of 1914, and in September 1939 saw even the bones in those hands turn to dust. Once that ''first stage'' was passed, Nivasio changed his mind. The further this collector of experiences has advanced into maturity, the more he has appreciated the benefits that his mental qualities, his habits, his knowledge of life have drawn from such ''natural'' contact with the privileged classes.

Geographically, the fringe of the Balkans belongs to Europe, but the natives of the region consider themselves, if not non-Europeans, then certainly Minor Europeans. From his acquaintance with the inferiority of others, Nivasio Dolcemare has drawn a wholesome superiority complex—the first benefit received from his accidental native land; added to which is the memory of epic mountains and heroic valleys, of clear and deep seas, of an ''earthly immortality'' presented in its most stable and comforting aspect.

This chosen society, this group of the elect, was referred to generically by the natives as ''the aristocracy.'' For the native, an ''aristocrat'' was anyone who belonged to the elect society, even if he lacked the certifications of blood and family. But within the elect society, the distinction between actual aristocrats and aristocrats by association was noted, commented on, anatomized. This fueled a continual ferment, a hostility, a fight without quarter, which, among the elect, was perhaps their most serious, their most heartfelt activity. Close attention was also paid to the distinction between old and new aristocrats, as well as between working and non-working aristocrats. One lady showed another lady her family's coat-of-arms. ''That little spot between the staves on the field of azure—is it perhaps a piece of soap?" the second lady asked the first, whose husband was an executive in the soap industry; and the question led to a long series of duels with pistol and sabre between the husbands and relatives of the two ladies. But these were mysteries of the temple. How could one tell "from outside" the necessary difference between people who were "born" and people who were "not born"? How, from beyond the gilded perimeter, could one penetrate the arcana of that happy and distant world? We can date to the same period the plebeian error that a man who is well-off is "living like a king."

The first quality of aristocratism, of every "aristism," of any optimum condition, is a natural faculty of synthesis. The "best" and the "most" are obtained with a minimum of effort, undetectable, and in the highest cases inexistent. Thus, in the supreme perfection of this equilibristic play, it is supposed that a man can acquire his own personal gravity, independent of the earth's gravity, and thereafter live in the air.

We think with ever-increasing urgency of the need for a superior biology, a moral biology, an intellectual biology: a precise science, an instrument of knowledge for a world that is inexistent as yet for the majority, is intuited by some, but in the vague, gelatinous manner of a limbo, and only for a very few is knowable and real. Then, in the light of the future "new science," will appear the perfect balance between the "maximums" attained by man within himself and outside of himself, the affinity between aristocracy and style, the partnership of excellences. And glancing over the past, it will be possible to measure, for example, the distance between the aristocratic mark of Picasso and the plebeian thickness of a good many crude paintings; between a slender triplet of Bellini and the obese harmonism, the toothless sonority of Wagner.

But we are speaking here of an epoch when values existed more as memories than as presences, more as appearances than as substantial realities. On the other hand, only one who has known that epoch which was no more than a charming stage set, is equipped to uncover without hesitation the truth of the present time: softness has given way to hardness, avoidance to collision, ambiguity to affirmation. Only one who has known Values reduced to pure memory can understand the full scope of the drama of Values today, their desperate will to power, their struggle for life.

The non-Europeanism of the natives, which the natives themselves acknowledged and thus presented as a given fact, favored the colonialist arrogance of the elect, the ostentatious superiority of the white to the black. Not that the natives in question were of Hamitic race, but the inequality of races is not always to be measured by the color of the skin.

At that time there was a flourishing market for a certain kind of pleated paper which, when manipulated by skillful hands, would turn itself into lampshades for sheltering and alleviating the light in those absurd drawing rooms with their forest-like gloom. But to see the *petticoat lampshade* as the only destiny of this pleated paper would be a mistake. Clandestinely, this paper served for packaging the final specimens of this "high-born" humanity, which had come to the last drops of its own story. Yet the elect, who had barely the consistency of the paper itself, these aristocrats whom the wind could blow through, preserved in the face of the plebeians an intact, magical, divine power. To command, to be obeyed, a word, a glance, the mere hint of a glance was enough. So far does habit survive the death of fact.

Equally admirable was the steadfastness with which the elect kept the virtues of their class alive. Scorn of danger: what matter if it was feigned? Daring: what matter if it was simulated? To be always the first to acknowledge the new, and accept it. Who if not they officially recognized the bicycle? On sultry summer afternoons, along paths white with gravel or grey with cinders, hour after hour rolled the aristocracy, even the women with their billowing bloomers, on shiny bicycles, in S's, figure-eights, circles, ovals, vying with each other in speed or slowness, with feet or without feet, with hands or without hands, straight-up or sidesaddle, the boldest occasionally coming to a "stand," the supreme triumph of skill, body erect on the pedals, front wheel swinging in the air, tranquil and magnificent.

Then one day the miracle exploded. Preceded by a golden hum, the Carriage of the Future made its first appearance. . . .

But that was already in Nivasio Dolcemare's lifetime.

Childhood of Nivasio Dolcemare

Childhood: in Italian, *infanzia,* a corruption of *Ninfanzia,* the period of his life a man spends under the authority of Anzia, the nymph of first fruits. (Anzia: from *ante,* first.)

I.

The day Nivasio Dolcemare issued from the maternal womb, the sun beat like a hammer on the city of the owl.

Tall, tinted tallow candles, five on one side and five on the other, emerged from the corners of the fireplace, leaning down from their bronze candlesticks, weeping long tears.

The cradle sparkled in a corner.

Every few moments a quick rustling of water ran down the walls and over the windows, which opposed their shut blinds to the assault of the prodigious heat.

This quick rustling suggested an intermittent rain, a weary rain, a ghostly rain. It was, however, the work of a dozen hired men, clad in wool from head to foot, who, under orders from Commendatore Visanio, poured buckets of water over the roof to ease the distress of the woman in labor beneath it.

The theme of water on the roof and above all of

candles burning in the daytime, nourished conversation in Casa Dolcemare for a long time afterwards.

The lady of the house, Signora Trigliona, received on Tuesdays. The friends of the Dolcemares lived in terror. It never failed that some careless or ingenuous person would suddenly blurt out:

"My, it's hot today!"

"Please!" Signora Trigliona would leap to her feet. "You have no idea what heat is! When I 'had' my little Nivasio . . ."

The episode of the candles was incorporated into Nivasio Dolcemare's life. When Thanatos had sealed the lips of Commendatore Visanio and Signora Trigliona, he took upon himself the task of preserving its memory, of handing it on to posterity, which he carried out as a sacred duty.

The mirror framed with gilded palms, which from the marble of the fireplace lifted its faded light to the stucco-encrusted ceiling, created an illusory continuation of that room filled with darkness and destiny, together with a happy anticipation of the fate of the unborn Nivasio, whose life, in fact, has been spent in a world of mirrors.

After this apodictic introduction, it will be easier to understand some of the ups and downs of Nivasio Dolcemare's destiny, to justify the reputation of being a *fils de famille* which has stuck to him like a crust, and which no one, least of all himself, has been able to say whether it has helped or hurt him.

For Nivasio Dolcemare, a timely determination of surroundings is more necessary than for others.

No one can tell what category this most "human" of men should be placed in. His social position escapes common judgment; it does not correspond to any of the usual classifications. Nor is his personal good will, his acknowledged modesty, enough to gain him normal acceptance.

If we think of people as little balls, seeing how sooner or later each little ball finds the right little hole to serve as its nest, we may be surprised by this one little ball, so like all the others and yet so different, which keeps rolling around and never comes to rest.

This is the drama of Nivasio Dolcemare. The singularity of other singular men speaks for itself, argues its own case, proves its worth. It is grand, conspicuous, ostentatious. Its proprietors nourish it carefully, oil it, polish it, take pains to make it ever more pleasing to the groundlings. Whims, flatteries, obstinacy, primitivism combine to make the singular man, the "superior" man, a successful and well-paid character. The singularity of Nivasio Dolcemare, on the other hand, is so discreet, so hidden, so subcutaneous, that nothing seeps out to the surface, and it is mistaken for the most excessive normality. But it is there, a hidden sea, and it surrounds this man-island with a desert-like zone, a belt of emptiness.

During the war, Nivasio Dolcemare was a soldier; a simple private. His discharge papers testify that "Private Dolcemare has served his country faithfully and with honor." Why then does he lack those tangible signs of faithfulness and honor with which his companions are so abundantly decorated?

In the confusion of the barracks, in the tumult of the field, the name of *Dolcemare Nivasio* occasionally rang out, and this name preceded by its surname sounded so strange that Nivasio himself used to listen to it with curiosity, as if it belonged to someone else, someone he did not know.

He hastened to answer the call anyway, and planted himself at attention in front of his "superior." He obeyed temporal authority, because submission of the body to temporal authority allows the spirit to remain free.

Faced with this soldier who looked so much like every other soldier, but whose metaphysical unlikeness showed through by obscure signs, the "superior" inevitably became inarticulate. He stared at Nivasio as if at a ghost that was moving about in disguise among the living. The mechanism of subordination went crazy. The superior felt that he had no control over Private Dolcemare. The classic "Dismissed" was hardly necessary to bring the impossible interview to an end.

Meanwhile, Private Dolcemare remained unutilized. It never occurred to anyone that this disinterested, absent-minded, inattentive foot soldier could be assigned the most absurd tasks, could be called upon for the highest sacrifice. No one ever understood that Private Dolcemare was *ready for anything*.

A foreigner in the ranks, would Nivasio Dolcemare have been more "at home" among the officers? No. As a general, Nivasio Dolcemare would have been forever "displaced."

In his own way, Nivasio Dolcemare is another victim of democracy. His case is far more tragic than that of a deposed monarch. Nivasio's lot is denied any possibility of change.

By nature, Nivasio should sit at the very top, breathing in the supreme solitude, contemplating the ultimate silence. But who will akcnowledge Nivasio Dolcemare's optical rights, his breathing privileges?

Otherwise ineffable, the "sovereignty" of Nivasio

Dolcemare is a reality for himself alone, a perpetual cause of imbalance, a perennial source of suffering.

Nivasio Dolcemare is another victim of democracy: not of democracy as it is framed in precise periods of history, but of the eternal, immutable democracy of mankind.

It was approaching noon; the silence deepened. In the growing tension of the genetic drama, Commendatore Visanio expected every moment to hear the cry of the sacred bird.

Prophetic sign!

In the mind of this athletic and adventurous Italian, ancient theogonic reminiscences and the traces of obscure superstitions had been fused into a little myth for personal use, according to which the birth of a son should be greeted from the summit of the Acropolis by the cry of the bird of Minerva, roused from its age-old sleep for the occasion. But either because the howls of Signora Trigliona drowned out every other sound, or because the blinds and hermetically sealed windows prevented any outside infiltration, Commendatore Visanio heard nothing.

Nivasio, too, considers it fortunate to be born under the azure eye of Athena, but not for the same reasons as a classicist, much less a neo-classicist.

Greece has been subjected more than once to the strange phenomenon of "decortication," which Plato mentions in the *Timaeus* and describes more fully in the *Critias*.

The "first" Greece was an extremely fertile land, which, with its shady forests, abundant fields, and babbling streams, combined in itself all magnificence and plenty.

One day this blessed skin came off like the skin of a snake and fell into the sea, leaving behind a bare, emaciated land.

This happened at the dawn of time, when Atlantis still flourished with its annular canals and the splendor of its gilded bronzes, but over such a long period, that is between the former age and today, the strange phenomenon has repeated itself, not in a physical but in a moral sense.

The St. Bartholomew of Europe, Greece, following this second denuding, became the geographical equivalent of the "flayed man" in anatomy.

Lacking qualities of its own, the Greece of today is the miniature model, the caricature, the "flayed man" of Europe. The character, and above all the weaknesses of the continent, which in their actual dimensions either deceive us or go unnoticed, stand out in the reduced model with such pitiless clarity and severity that any hope of mistaking them is vain.

He who knows Greece knows Europe, not in its illusions, its pretensions, its "mysteries," but in its poor and bare truth.

Before entering into life as a disguised ghost, Nivasio Dolcemare had looked into an infallible mirror, he had spent a season in hell.

Which is why, in the course of this biographical documentation, the *Italian* Nivasio Dolcemare will give evidence of a vision so cold and lucid as to inspire uneasiness, if not horror.

While waiting to put her hands in the dough, the midwife crawled around the room on her knees, invoking heavenly authority:

> Patience help us,
> Christ provide for us,
> There's only thirteen of us
> And hard times for all.

The midwife had an auspicious name: she was called Zoé.

Bimba, the forty-year-old sister of the mother-to-be, stuffed her ears with cotton and hid in the linen closet.

As an Italian born outside of Italy, Nivasio Dolcemare considers himself privileged.

This "indirect" birth is an ironic situation, a stylistic solution, a condition that has added certain nuances, certain subtleties, certain half- and quarter-tone passages to the national faculties of the man Dolcemare which "direct" birth would not have permitted.

The birth of an Italian outside of Italy is the equivalent of a veiled painting or recorded music. It is, in the problem of race, the attainment of style.

Analysis of the Italian Nivasio Dolcemare concludes: he is a more Italian Italian than the ordinary Italian, because the "Italian" in him is not a "local situation" but a willed condition, a discovery, a conquest.

Which is not to say that the condition of being an Italian born outside of Italy has not brought him a few unpleasant surprises as well.

In May, 1915, Nivasio Dolcemare arrived from abroad in the railway station of Turin. He was directed to a little table next to the arrival gate, behind which sat a plump, good-natured colonel, a paterfamilias in uniform.

The colonel said, "Greetings," and took the papers that Dolcemare held out to him.

"Born in Athens? You're a Greek, then! What are you poking into our mess for?"

Nivasio Dolcemare looked up. He saw, looming

through the smoke-filled station, an Italy with a tower on its head. And this Italy—who knows why?—was laughing up its sleeve.

"Murderer!"

Commendatore Visanio appeared tragically in the doorway, his eyes flashing at Doctor Naso, who stood, gloomy and preoccupied, swinging a long purple gut between his legs like a bell, as if he were about to smash it against the wall.

"Murderer! You've killed my son!"

But before the Commendatore's fist could land on the doctor's head, a piercing cry rang out.

The long-awaited cry of the owl . . . ? Wrong. The cry of a throttled rooster . . . ? Wrong again. It was the first cry of Nivasio Dolcemare.

Among the many thoughts that flowed loosely through his head, Commendatore Visanio asked himself why the birth of a child is called a "joyous event," but was unable to find a satisfactory answer.

"Commendatore, see if you can be of help in there," Doctor Naso implored.

To correct his earlier mistake, Commendatore Visanio burst into activity, moved furniture, opened drawers, closed them again, wheeled the medicine table through the room, hid himself in a cloud like Jove.

"Stop, Commendatore!"

The leg of the medicine table had caught on the rug: a brown, caustic stain of tincture of iodine spread over the Bokhara.

The zeal of the new father threatened worse woes. Doctor Naso pumped anti-hemorrhage fluid from a small vial.

"Doctor, why is the birth of a child called a 'joyous event'?"

The doctor gave him a blank look and went on injecting extract of bearded rye into the veins of Signora Trigliona.

"Signora Zoé . . ."

"Sit down," the midwife ordered.

On one of those boat-shaped divans that furnish the paintings of Watteau, Commendatore Visanio witnessed the handling of the newborn.

Cleaned and decked out like a fine ham, little Nivasio sank into the foam of the cradle.

Signora Trigliona fell asleep. Her emptied body flattened out on the bed; her hands, resting on the sheet, could be distinguished from it only by the slight shadow surrounding them.

Doctor Naso and Signora Zoé left together. Once again, even amid the anxieties of childbirth, Commendatore Visanio asked himself if there might not be something between Naso and the midwife. An odor of disinfectant, an invisible wing of cleanliness, flitted through the room.

Why *is* the birth of a child called a "joyous event"?

Left alone, Commendatore Visanio became aware that he, too, had a body to look after, needs to be satisfied, and he was amazed.

In that moment, he underwent a "birth" of his own.

The sleep accumulated over two white nights suddenly confronted him and landed a blow on his head.

He was still on the couch that the midwife had confined him to. His foot, shod in an elastic-sided riding boot, dismounted from one of the armrests, dangling tragically in emptiness. His bearded centaur's head fell back on the cushions.

Then, in the thick silence, over the city numbed by heat, a cry resounded.

The Commendatore had plunged into the stony sleep of Holofernes. His lips showed red through the grimness of his beard, opening and closing rhythmically, kissing the void.

The cry came again. A sourceless, sexless cry. Round and sharp at the same time, enchanting and yet terrifying.

Commendatore Visanio did not hear the cry.

His enormous hand, palm up, creased with a capital M, lay on the floor like a glove. Between the trouser-leg pulled up on his calf and his sock which had collapsed like an accordion, the ribbon of his long drawers, tied at the ankle, stuck out a pair of rabbit's ears.

The cry came a third time.

But if the Commendatore had heard it, and had wanted to take it for the auspicious cry of the goddess, he would have thought, so far was this cry from any reality, that the bird of Minerva was as big as an ox.

II.

On Thursday, the twelfth of November, Commendatore Visanio and Signora Trigliona celebrated with great pomp the baptism of little Nivasio.

Nivasio was baptized in the chapel of Casa Dolcemare, at four in the afternoon, by the Archbishop himself.

Monsignor Delenda placed salt on the lips of the new soldier of Christ and baptized him in the name of the Father, the Son, and the Holy Spirit.

An adagio by Palestrina, transcribed for solo strings, came floating in from the drawing room, performed by the ladies' orchestra of the "Mon Plaisir," under the direction of Deolinda Zimbalist.

In tactful reference to the sex of the baptized one, Deolinda Zimbalist and her ladies were dressed uniformly in sky-blue satin. Down the ribbons that diagonally crossed the players' breasts, the words *Wiener-damen* were written in gold letters.

At the end of the austere rite, the celebration began in the most brilliant fashion.

Notable among those present were Count Minciaki, minister plenipotentiary of H. M. the Emperor of Austria, doyen of the diplomatic corps, and the Countess; *Monsieur de Roujoux,* minister plenipotentiary of the French Republic, and *Madame de Roujoux;* Baron von Rathibor, minister plenipotentiary of H. M. the Emperor of Germany, and the Baroness; Prince Vassilchikov, minister plenipotentiary of H. M. the Emperor of Russia, and the Princess, née Baroness von Klübert; General Papatrapatakos, commander of the Athenian garrison, and the Generaless; Prefect Tsapatakalakis, and the Prefectress; Mayor Pestromastranzoglu, and the Mayoress; Antoine Calaroni; the director of the gas company; and many others.

The refreshments were prepared by Armand Loubié et Fils, purveyors to the Royal Household.

The guests spoke in French, with a Levantine accent.

Antoine Calaroni was the pillar of the drawing rooms. His presence at receptions in Athenian high society was as necessary as salt in the kitchen.

The comparison should not be taken literally. Calaroni was the most insipid man in the world, but no one more perfectly combined in himself the three cardinal virtues of the man of the world: decorative ugliness, amiable stupidity, and self-assured ignorance.

Antoine Calaroni frequented the drawing rooms with regularity and devotion, as a believer frequents the house of God. His reputation for being "the most faithful" was unchallenged.

When the orchestra of Viennese ladies made its debut at the "Mon Plaisir," Deolinda Zimbalist received inside a bunch of violets the visiting card of Antoine Calaroni, ex-honorary consul of the Republic of Guatemala; and from that night on, regularly, the faithful Calaroni continued to send his floral homage to "the divine, the incomparable . . ."

There was a certain affinity between Antoine Calaroni and Stendhal. The same woman who refused nothing to other men, would barely allow Calaroni to kiss the tip of her finger. But Antoine was just as happy with that. He was happy. He had discovered the least hazardous way of being happy, and he maintained it with great constancy.

Calaroni was a virgin.

Firearms, which play such an important part in the development of a virile character, filled him with unspeakable horror.

Apart from the love of Signora Calaroni, his mother, Antoine never knew the love of any other woman. But for his mother, whom no one in the city remembered any longer because she had been dead from time immemorial, Calaroni entertained a love even beyond love: a cult.[1]

He was an ageless innocent. Very old men, like General Papatrapatakos, commander of the garrison, could not remember Calaroni ever looking any different: the same thin, ebony moustache, the same side-whiskers, the same vacuous eyes floating in a perpetual humidity, the same wrinkles around the corners of the mouth, which lent to the cadaverous smile of this untilled humus the stamp of immortality.

By nature denied any form of manual or mental activity, Calaroni possessed a single skill: embroidery. In the labors of Arachne, Antoine was a master. His fine lines, his cross-stitches and chain-stitches were inimitable masterworks. Which paled, however, before the great compositions, the sumptuous tapestries rich with pastoral creatures, foaming brooks, woodcocks, that Calaroni worked at yearlong in the mystery of his solitary and inviolable lodgings, and with which he paid homage at Christmastime to the ladies whose hospitality he had enjoyed throughout the year.

The celebration started off with a choice program of music, performed by the ladies' orchestra. Deolinda Zimbalist drew applause as soloist in a rhapsody by Wieniawski. The director of the gas company, Oscar Dacosta, who had a fine bass voice, sang the aria "Et moi-même je serais ton bourreau . . . ," from *La Juive*.

Finally, under the direction of Deolinda Zimbalist, who partly played and partly beat time with her bow, the ladies' orchestra gave a brilliant rendition of the famous *Poet and Peasant* overture.

With the last chords, the guest of honor arrived in the drawing room. His little head was embedded in lace. He screwed up his eyes in the light; drool ran from his innocent little mouth.

"He's his father all over!" exclaimed Countess Minciaki.

"He has his mother's nose!" Madame de Roujoux retorted.

Nivasio burped, farted, and generally behaved so indecorously that he had to be taken away again without further ado.

The shrieks of the guest of honor had not quite ceased behind the red velvet curtains when Deolinda Zimbalist thrust out her chest, took the trembling bow in her vigorous hand, and with the boldness of a lion-tamer led her ladies to the attack in "O mein liebe

Augustin." To the unleashed rhythm of the mazurka, the dancing was begun by Commendatore Visanio, in whose robust arms, which longed for quite different embraces, the old Countess Minciaki, doyenne of the diplomatic corps, bounced up and down.

The table for *maus* had been set up in the yellow drawing room, but there were no players.

Mikos and Takos, two inseparable octogenarians, sat at a small table apart playing double solitaire. Loud voices could be heard in the adjacent ballroom. Suddenly, amid the hoarse shouts of Captain Tsitsipitikakis, commander of the lancers, the shrill voice of Generaless Papatrapatakos rang out:

"The Vianellis!"

Mikos and Takos looked at each other, appalled.

"The Vianellis?" stammered Mikos.

"The Vianellis!" confirmed Takos.

The festive noise gave way to an anxious murmur, an alarmed psst-psst.

Mikos and Takos rose from their table and rushed on wobbly legs for the door; but they had barely reached the threshold of the yellow drawing room when the lights suddenly went out.

"Mikos!" cried Takos.

"Takos!" cried Mikos. And they groped for each other in the darkness.

Casa Dolcemare stood facing Constitution Square, and facing the same square stood the house of the Vianellis.

They were scandalous women.

Arturo Vianelli, an importer of colonial commodities, had died three years earlier, leaving his wife and daughters without a cent to their names.

The orphans were two big, buxom girls, two triumphant creatures, two splendid examples of womanhood, who, when they entered the Catholic church in Athens on a Sunday morning, made even the statue of St. Dionysius the Areopagite, to whom the church was dedicated, poke its head from the niche, its eyes glowing like lanterns. As for the widow, the mother of the two orphans, she was endowed with such perfections as to tempt even the sternest appraiser.

The mother Vianelli, who was received in society with a certain sympathy while poor Arturo was alive, saw the doors close one by one in her face after she was left a widow.

The house of the Vianellis was pointed at by the puritans of the city, and when crossing Constitution Square, families would take a wide turn around that hot-bed of depravity.

In the wee hours, the blinds of Casa Vianelli still emitted a ripple of song, a rustling of guitars. Casa Vianelli was frequented in the evenings by officers from the garrison and from the fleet anchored in the bay.

Mothers of marriageable daughters were most incensed against "those strumpets," and among the fiercest was the Generaless Papatrapatakos, whose daughter Pipizza, breastless and chlorotic, was at that time, and in the most perfect conditions of nubility, just rounding the cape of forty.

From the window of the Dolcemare drawing room, the Generaless had seen the Vianellis, mother and daughters, leave their house and cross the square in the direction of Casa Dolcemare, and, aware of the danger, had given the alarm.

Anything could be expected from such shameless women. Who knows if, profiting from little Nivasio's baptism, they might not try to violate the confines of Casa Dolcemare?

Signora Trigliona summoned Pelopidas, her major-domo, had the lights turned off, gave the necessary orders.

"Pelopidas," said Signora Trigliona, "when those people ring, inform them that the mistress is not at home."

Great was the expectation in the darkness, behind the window curtains. The Generaless Papatrapatakos acted as lookout, and communicated the enemy's movements to those behind her.

The Vianellis crossed the square, passed by the gates of Casa Dolcemare, and continued on their way.

No one breathed. The lights were turned on again.

"En avant deux!" cried Captain Tsitsipitikakis in his hoarse commander's voice, rescuing his lancers from the general consternation.

Dejected, Mikos and Takos went back to their game of double solitaire.

While these events were taking place on the ground floor, on the floor above, in a room clad in light blue, Nivasio was sucking at the swollen breast of Mitrulla, who on her native Delos, the floating island of Diana and Apollo, had been put in a motherly way by Sophocles, the long-haired evzone.

Five years later.

Deolinda Zimbalist is still directing the orchestra of the "Mon Plaisir," but the "Mon Plaisir' is no longer so.

Where are the successes of old, the applause, the cheers? Deolinda puts more dash and fire into her interpretations than ever, but to what avail? With the passing years, the beautiful Deolinda's admirers gradually drifted away.

In his distress, Signor Stómachos, proprietor of the establishment, has come to believe that between the admirers of Deolinda and the clients of the "Mon Plaisir" there can be no solution of continuity.

It is springtime. A magnificent evening.

The elite pour into the "Cocorico," where Tiarko and his gypsy orchestra are playing.

The same ones who only yesterday knew no other idol than Deolinda Zimbalist, now raise to the stars this olive-colored fiddler in his lion-tamer's costume, this Magyar with the spring and sinuosity of a great carnivore, this hairy tyrant who beats his women with the brass-studded belt that holds up his pants.

There are whispers that among the beaten is Princess Vassilchikov herself, née Baroness von Klübert and nicknamed among her intimates "Nadya the Insatiable."

Antoine Calaroni enters the "Mon Plaisir." The room is brightly lit and deserted. Calaroni is dressed in a grey three-piece suit with tails, a top hat of the same grey, white spats, a monocle on a ribbon, pale gloves with black stitching, and carries an Indian cane. In his right hand he holds a bouquet of flowers, which will soon lie at the feet of the "divine," the "incomparable."

Nicomedes crosses the room and places on Calaroni's table a glass and a half bottle of mineral water—

the only drink acceptable to this man of the world who has seen so much.

In a corner, Mikos and Takos, the inseparable octogenarians, are playing their game of double solitaire. The waves of "The Blue Danube" fill the sparkling, empty room with vain rumblings, with glittering lunacy.

Old Nicomedes leans down to Calaroni.

"Do you remember, Signor Antoine, when this waltz used to set the whole house singing?"

Calaroni nods. Nicomedes leans closer to him.

"Those two old men, Mikos and Takos, offered to pay if they could play their game in silence."

"You are not by any chance going to dismiss the orchestra?" Calaroni asks, deeply troubled.

"Stómachos doesn't want to. He says if he has to die, he will die on his feet."

At midnight, Deolinda and Antoine leave the "Mon Plaisir." The shutters roll down behind them with a bang. The night is cool. Deolinda holds her violin case tightly under her arm; inside her cloak of imitation leopard skin she clutches the flowers of "the most faithful."

The pier is deserted. The moon is high and spreads a silver carpet on the water.

"If the 'Mon Plaisir' closes at the end of the month, what will you do?"

"I don't know," Deolinda replies. "Perhaps I'll go home to Pilsen."

They walk on in silence. They stop in front of Milonas's boarding house, where La Zimbalist lives.

In the darkness, Antoine seeks the violinist's hand.

"If you had wished, Deolinda . . ."

La Zimbalist looks at the moon shining on the sea.

A bit of that shining is reflected in her eyes. Or perhaps it is a tear.

"If you had wished . . ."

"Ach! Be quiet, Antoine! Why are you always digging up the past?"

And she adds, to Schumann's melody:

"*Warum*?"

Neither speaks for a long time. Calaroni's spats shine white against the sidewalk; the monocle flashes in his eye. Bowed by an elegant affliction, his ageless body leans over the knob of his Indian cane, in the posture of the Apollo *savrocthonos.*

"*Atieu,*" sighs Deolinda.

"No, not good-bye, but *aurevoir,*" murmurs Calaroni.

He turns to leave, but a sudden thought stops him.

"By the way, I ran into Dolcemare this morning. He has such odd ideas! He wants his son to learn German! He is looking for a respectable, well-educated person, a tutor, to live with the family. If any of your acquaintances . . ."

"My acquaintances?" Deolinda repeats mechanically. "I who am bereft of acquaintances . . . ?"

Pause.

"But I will think about it. My dear friend, please tell Commendatore Dolcemare that Signora Zimbalist will think about it."

Deolinda descended the first step.

Under the violinless violinist's instruction, Nivasio Dolcemare would recite before going to bed, in a voice filled with sleep:

Ein zwei
Polizei

Drei vier
Grenadier
Fünf sechs
Alte Hex
Sieben acht
Gute Nacht.

After the first step, Deolinda descended a second.

Not only did she initiate little Nivasio into the less profound principles of German prosody, but she also took him for walks, gave him his bath, sat him on the chamber pot, wiped his bottom.

At this point occurs Nivasio Dolcemare's first act of pride, and the consequent punishment.

It was morning and the air was translucent. Nivasio happened to be alone in the playroom when an acute rectal stimulus forced him to put off the difficult construction of a castle of blocks.

He went to the door to call Frau Deolinda, but before giving voice he thought: "I am a man. I must be self-reliant. Today begins a new life."

He took the chamber pot from the commode and placed it in the middle of the room, pulled down his shorts and underpants which fell around his feet, and backed resolutely towards the receptacle.

But as he approached and tried to get the chamber pot under him so that he could sit on it, the chamber pot kept moving, pushed away by Nivasio's shorts which were stretched between his feet.

The stimulus grew more acute. Nivasio could no longer restrain the dilation of his sphincter, and what had to happen happened.

Nivasio jumped back. He saw in the middle of the polished floor a little part of himself, a dark little twirl holding up a steaming point; and his grief was such that he burst into tears.

The altered social condition of Deolinda Zimbalist produced in the new governess an equally great physical and moral alteration. Her very name fell to the demands of brachyphony, and Deolinda Zimbalist became *Frau Linda.*

The ex-violinist grew so ungainly that her body, which in the days of the "Mon Plaisir" emanated a delicate scent of iris,[2] now exhaled a diffuse malodor of kerosene. The similarity between Frau Linda's smell and the smell of kerosene was Nivasio Dolcemare's discovery. Nivasio Dolcemare's sense of smell is still very keen, but in his childhood it was simply phenomenal. At that time, men and women were nothing but ambulatory odors for him. "Camphor," "belladonna," "spit on a hot iron" corresponded to so many flesh-and-blood persons.[3] Nivasio could smell a chair, an armchair, or a divan and say who had been sitting in it an hour earlier. The Tuesday receptions left abandoned canes, umbrellas, gloves in the entryway of Casa Dolcemare: Nivasio would smell the object and name without hesitation the person it belonged to.

By a strange contradiction, Frau Linda's neglect of personal hygiene developed together with an intense microphobia. The fear of death by poisoning tortured the governess. At table, Frau Linda warily scrutinized the food. She would push her plate away, crying out *"Smuzig! Smuzig!"*[4] She touched doorknobs only with a corner of her dress protecting her hand. Her life, which once soared on the wings of music, now sank into the gloomiest matter.

Inside even the mildest of men there sleeps a tyrant. In the arrangement drawn up between Commendatore Visanio and Deolinda Zimbalist, the sleeping tyrant whispered to Commendatore Visanio the clause that "during her stay in Casa Dolcemare, Signora Zimbalist will not play the violin."

Shut up in its wooden coffin and stored under the governess's bed, the glorious instrument slowly died of silence. Four sharp twangs some months apart broke the stillness of the night. Four times Frau Linda jumped up in bed and fell back moaning to the mattress. Like the lyre of Orpheus, the violin of her who had been the beautiful Zimbalist lay with broken strings.

In the afternoon, Frau Linda used to take Nivasio to the Zappeion gardens, which face the arid Aegean, with the Acropolis on the right and on the left Mount Hymettos, which is the color of its honey.

It was in the Zappeion gardens that the idyll between Frau Linda and Claas van der Hoderaa blossomed. Nivasio collaborated in this romance as an innocent messenger, because the letters in which the quartermaster of Vlaardingen declared his love to Frau Linda were consigned to Nivasio, who consigned them in turn to the governess.

The sky was radiant. A youthful breeze ruffled the white clouds, curled back the locks of the Aegean. A row of young cypresses crowned the hill of the Cemetery, that hill up which, in a few years, Commendatore Visanio would go to his final rest.

It was the season of love, the season of sailors. But that afternoon, Claas van der Hoderaa gave no sign of life. In recompense, if there could be any recompense, Frau Linda and Nivasio met General Papatrapatakos striding boldly among the flower beds with his chest puffed out and his hands behind his back, his walking stick hanging between his legs like an afflicted tail.

His Excellency only recognized people when they came nose to nose, but then he would break out in loud exclamations of surprise. When His Excellency recognized his "little friend" Nivasio, he uttered his usual cries of amazement, then pinched his cheek with a hand accustomed to leading troops to victory, and finally asked him:

"What will you be when you grow up?"

Nivasio stared at the tips of his boots and replied in a muffled voice:

"A priest."

His Excellency uttered a roar of amazement.

"A priest?"

He let out a huge laugh.

"A priest!"

He turned to Deolinda.

"Did you hear that? A priest!"

Deolinda looked at the general without batting an eye and said:

"A child's heart is a shrine of mistizismus."

General Papatrapatakos, who thanks to the sacerdotal ambitions of Nivasio Dolcemare had hoped to broach a long conversation with the still charming Deolinda Zimbalist, was annihilated by her reply. He stared at the governess, turned in a huff and disappeared among the flower beds.

Nivasio Dolcemare not only did not become a priest, but the only deity he recognizes is the goddess Intelligence. This might be the place to examine the cause of this diversion. But was it a diversion? Was it not rather a conversion?

Nivasio Dolcemare sought God for a long time. His heart for many years could not decide between the Catholic God and the Greek God. In the end, the Greek God prevailed. Why?

The Catholic church in Athens is dedicated to St. Dionysius the Areopagite. It is a bright, cold building. The apse was decorated by the last of the Baroque masters, Ermengildo Buonfiglioli, who came to Greece expressly at the invitation of Monsignor Delenda, the Catholic Archbishop of Athens.

In those same years, Paul Cézanne was beginning to be talked about, but his name had not yet reached the ears of Monsignor Delenda, and it is to be feared that the prelate went to his heavenly reward ignorant not only of the work but of the very name of the painter from Aix.

Unaware of the revolution that was shaking the art of painting at that time, mindful of the fame of the great fresco painters, Monsignor Delenda entrusted the decoration of the apse of St. Dionysius the Areopagite to Ermengildo Buonfiglioli, in whom, it was said, the tradition of the Umbrian school was continued.

It might be inferred from the foregoing that Nivasio Dolcemare is a Cézannian. Wrong. Not only is Nivasio Dolcemare not a Cézannian, but he showed magnificent courage in stemming the epidemic of Cézannism that devastated Europe in the first quarter of the century and continues, in part, to devastate it; was prophetic in his discovery and stormy denunciation of the negative qualities of such painting.

All the same, especially considering the cloud that surrounded him, Cézanne had the merit of discovering, or better of rediscovering, a fundamental principle of painting, which is that painting is not a reproduction of the real. And that, particularly when portraying the human figure, one must leave instead of the face a neutral oval to which the viewer can imaginatively attach the face of a friend, a relative, the lady of his dreams, or whomever he likes; or else go so deeply into the reality of the subject as to produce a sort of intellectual radiograph of him.

We have thus good reason to believe that if the apse of the church of St. Dionysius the Areopagite had been painted not by Ermengildo Buonfiglioli but by Paul Cézanne, Nivasio Dolcemare would most probably not have opted for the Greek God, and today—who knows?—he might be a famous theologian, a courageous missionary, perhaps even a Prince of the Church.

That evening, General Papatrapatakos appeared earlier than usual in the Potato Club. The main table for *maus* was already full. Seated around the green cloth were Count Minciaki, Captain Tsitsipitikakis, Oscar Dacosta, director of the gas company, among others.

His Excellency attacked without delay.

"I must tell you something extraordinary. I run into little Dolcemare today and ask him what he wants to be when he grows up. Do you know what he says?"

The players take their noses from their cards, gaze kindly at the general, and replied in one voice:

"A priest."

The attraction that priesthood exercised on the childhood of Nivasio Dolcemare can be ascribed in part to what is secret, closed, "dark" *even* in a priest's clothing.

In the earliest years of his childhood, Nivasio wore

his hair in long curls, and his parents dressed him like a girl.

In his little wardrobe there reigned a princess of yellow silk with a high waist and balloon sleeves that left the arms exposed.

This shameful costume aroused violent reactions in the little male, and while Nivasio, encumbered and humiliated, twisted his arms behind his back to hide them from mortifying glances, his exasperated soul aspired to the cassock[5] with its countless black buttons, as to a secure sheath that would enclose him completely.

But Nivasio's obscure animosity was not taken into consideration either by Commendatore Visanio or by Signora Trigliona. Childhood, which is austere, fateful, and far more venerable than old age, was for them a "little puppet world," that is, according to etymology, a world of dolls.

It is a miracle, then, that despite the heedlessness of Commendatore Visanio, and the futility of Signora Trigliona, and the sotadic influence of the scandalous princess, Nivasio Dolcemare has not enriched with his presence the already crowded ranks of inversion.

Let us pause briefly over this word, the name of one of the most discussed and preoccupying anomalies of life.

With regard to inversion, Nivasio Dolcemare entertains no moral prejudices, still less any male pride. For its effects on certain intellective faculties, he considers inversion not only innocent but even, in a sense, favorable. At the end of the varied paths mankind is following, the sleeping Hermaphroditus represents today, as in the time of the *Symposium,* the ideal image of perfection. He is not a divine neuter, however, but the divine all-in-all. And it is precisely in the name of Hermaphroditus that Nivasio Dolcemare denounces inversion, that great solitarity, as an enemy of perfection. He says:

"Art, gentlemen, which is the only activity that interests us, is not merely prayer, dedication, offering, but above all a taking possession, an act of conquest, a willed, imperative, triumphant construction. . . ."

A Voice: "Of what?"

The Speaker: "Of our Paradise!"

(Prolonged hurrahs, fanfares, a victory march gradually drifting away on the sea.)

Priesthood is, on the other hand, the most legitimate, the most obvious way of showing oneself to be superior to other men. Next comes the practice of arms, then political authority, artistic fame, the power of money, and finally, for the very few, there remains the practice of pure Intelligence. Here man no longer represents "a" superiority but superiority "itself."[6]

It is natural, then, that Nivasio Dolcemare, who from the first flickers of consciousness has felt the spur of a superior destiny, should have begun with an aspiration to priesthood, to arrive in the end at the practice—oh, how thankless!—of pure Intelligence.

Sometimes Nivasio Dolcemare yielded to his "basest pride." He flattered himself with belonging to the Catholic Church, because at the heart of the City of Orthodoxy, in the face of the natives, the church of St. Dionysius the Areopagite represented Europe, its Cannons, its Machines, its Progress. As he climbed the steps of the temple of Western Religion, Nivasio Dolcemare shamelessly savored the superiority of the White to the Black.

When his Greek friends wanted to humiliate him (and what other sentiment rules the fraternities of little men?), they would refer not to the Catholic, or Universal, Church, but to the Western Church, meaning the Declining Church. They intended to oppose light, triumphant and filled with future, to the twilight of defeat and approaching death. But the opposition of East to West, to which they joined the opposition of South to North, did not humiliate Nivasio Dolcemare. On the contrary. The opposition turned, instead, against his adversaries. No sign had yet appeared of that Decline of the West which some years later would inspire the Vichism of Spengler, and Nivasio clearly sensed that the very virtues extolled in the East and the South: the splendor of the sun, the absence of the dismal rigors of winter, the "perpetual smile of nature," constituted rather a state of inferiority, a shameful condition. *Ex oriente lux* can have meaning only for astronomy.

What more authoritative acknowledgment could there be of the superiority of the Western Church? Queen Olga herself, who in her dual quality of Russian princess and queen of Greece was Orthodox twice over, turned to the Catholic Church for what she found lacking in the Greek Church: grace of mind and verbal elegance. During Lent, wrapped in a black cape, her eyes hidden behind dark glasses, propped on the elbow of the aged Messalá, court master-of-ceremonies and "keeper of the keys," and while her august consort, George I, was being initiated into the mysteries of the French can-can by the priestesses of the Moulin Rouge, Olga Romanova, Queen of Greece, climbed the steps of the Catholic temple to hear the good word spread by the preachers who took turns in the pulpit of St. Dionysius the Areopagite, presided over by the Abbé Brémond, French academician and author of *L'Histoire littéraire du sentiment religieux.*

On Sundays, at eleven o'clock mass, Mighty Europe, in the form of the full diplomatic corps, met in the church of St. Dionysius the Areopagite. These Minciakis, these Rathibors, these Dukes of A., were not ardent believers; their presence at the foot of the altar was a political act, an official duty, a tonal chord in the Concert of Europe.

Each legation had its own mahogany pew enclosed by little gates, with seats and kneeling cushions upholstered in red velvet. As did the notable families.

The Roujoux family, composed of papa, mama, and four skinny and extremely ugly daughters, formed an edifying picture in the pew of the French legation. At the time, the fate of France was in the hands of the notorious Combes, the latest embodiment of the Antichrist, and if Monsieur de Roujoux had not yet attained the rank of Ambassador to which his merits and seniority entitled him, it was because of his unconcealed monarchical sentiments and his open adherence to the Church.

Equally edifying was the spectacle of the Marquise de Riancourt and her son Raul. They did not enjoy the privilege of a pew, but had two kneeling-chairs of carved walnut with red fringe around the arm-rests. This blue-blooded lady had abandoned France in an act of protest against the law of congregations, and moved to Athens where she was received at court and in the best society and kept open house. Obedient to the will of his mama, the Marquis Raul took Hellenic citizenship, after which he was called to serve under the banners of General Papatrapatakos.

The Marquise de Riancourt was blind. She walked with her stately head held high, her wide eyes veiled with a white membrane, her nostrils flared seeking her way on the wind, and she had a tendency to get lost. But she did not get lost, because the Marquis Raul, Antigone to her Oedipus, clung to her side, dressed in the uniform of the Greek infantry, steered her with his arm, and corrected her course.

Thanks to the diligent and extremely loving care of her son, the Marquise de Riancourt did not live the secluded, static life[7] to which blindness might reasonably have reduced her, but was present everywhere, at festivities, in the theaters, at receptions, and by authority presided over every gathering. Mother and son seemed joined by indissoluble bonds, united by an ineffable membrane. They pulled their oar in concert,[8] helped along by a pious little wind.

Though he was highly marriageable, the Marquis Raul was the laughingstock of the entire feminine consortium of Athenian high society. The young ladies called him *blakas,* which means "imbecile." Even the most marriage-hungry girls, the most voracious spinsters made fun of him; they set off firecrackers under his chair, and once threw his straw boater into a tree, from which they brought it down again with a hail of stones, reduced to a topless rim. At dinner they would mix cigar ashes in his wine, and enjoyed watching him get up from the table, pale and sweaty, under the stern and anxious gaze of his mother, and go out falteringly in search of the nearest sink. Those who are surprised by this reference to the Marquise de Riancourt's *gaze* should understand that a mother can "see" her own son even if she is blind.

The Marquise and Raul always arrived together. Once the Marquise was settled in the place of honor,

Titi, Fifi, and Nini, the cruelest, the most ruthless and seductive of the girls, would carry the chaste Raul off in a gay farandole, hide him behind a screen, in the shade of a *ficus elastica,* and tempt him like a new St. Anthony. "Raul!" the metallic voice of the Marquise would ring out, her milky eyes looking to the left, while the beseiged virgin was somewhere to her right. "Coming, mother!" the blank voice replied. "Here!" the jeweled index finger, brandished like a pick, pointed repeatedly at the carpet. And Raul, escaping his seducers, would take a chair and sit down to the left of the place of honor, his knees pressed together as if he were suffering from colic, his hands folded in his lap.

But one day the Marquise, more equine, yellow, stiff, and inquisitorial than ever, was seen taking her morning constitutional with military strides under the pepper trees of Queen Amelia Street, on the arm of an unknown woman dressed in the uniform of the Salvation Army. The news spread in a flash. What had become of Raul? Was he sick? In disgrace? The truth became known only several days later, and it was terrible. Raul de Riancourt had broken the maternal cord, deserted the banners of General Papatrapatakos, and run away to France with the prima donna of a light opera company who had been the rage at the Falero Theater all summer, beseiged in vain by the gilded youth of the capital: the unforgettable Suzon in *Madame Angot's Daughter,* the beautiful Ricordó. And not only had he run off with this "marionette," as the whole city was saying, but the moment they landed in Marseilles, he married her. A fearful lesson for all mothers of male children.

In a pew much too large for such a tiny, trembling couple, Count and Countess Minciaki justified the nickname of Philemon and Baucis which the "European" society of Athens had sympathetically given them.

Baroness von Rathibor always came alone, dressed in black, a missal clutched to her macerated martyr's breast. Everyone knew that the Baroness was pious, that she practiced charity efficiently and without ostentation, that "that brute of a Rathibor was no match for her in any respect."

Shortly before the elevation of the host, the imperious heel of the Baron would echo on the marble floor. Rathibor would march down the aisle of the church, throw open the little gate to his pew, looking neither right nor left, and plant himself upright next to his kneeling wife. When the bell of the elevation rang a few moments later, and all knees bent and heads bowed, he remained erect. Straight-backed, stern-browed, steely-eyed, arms crossed over his broad chest, Baron Hermann von Rathibor, a living statue of pride, looked down from his two meters' height upon the devotions of a kneeling people.

The solitude of the Duke of A. in the pew of the Italian legation was variously commented on. The Duchess returned under the conjugal roof only for brief, widely spaced visits. It was known that the rest of the time, drunk with happiness, she rushed about the splendid capitals of the West in the company of a Roman prince. The Duke was sad, dignified, extremely tight-lipped. The marital misadventures of that blue-blooded Sicilian were so well known that Nivasio himself, despite the fact that Commendatore Visanio and Signora Trigliona avoided "certain topics" in his presence, saw in his imagination a pair of tall, branching horns rising from the Duke of A.'s forehead, which transformed the diplomat into a living hatrack.

But this St. Hubert's vision was not enough to deliver Nivasio from the boredom that tormented him. In the noble pew of the Dolcemare family, Nivasio wriggled like a worm, stretched like a rubber band, swallowed yawns.

The apse painted by Ermengildo Buonfiglioli depicted with Tiepolesque rondures the ascension of St. Dionysius the Areopagite. The holy teacher rose to his heavenly reward supported at the elbows by four muscular cherubs, while other equally robust cherubs blew trumpets, mouthed cornets, beat drums, embraced cellos.

To escape the boredom inspired by the diplomatic corps kneeling in the pews, Nivasio lifted his eyes to the frescoes of Ermengildo Buonfiglioli; but in the Lord God seated on a cloud he met Count Minciaki with his handsome spade beard; in St. Dionysius the Areopagite he encountered Antoine Calaroni; in Our Lord Jesus Christ he recognized the "beau" Léon Mela, who each year at midnight mass sang in his warm baritone:

Minuit, chrétiens,
C'est l'heure solennelle. . . .

Though Nivasio had as yet no very clear notion of the metaphysics of art, this Paradise, which was simply an extension of the same society of whose fathomless vacuity and incommensurable idiocy he learned more each day, did not convince him.

Ermengildo Buonfiglioli ended his honest life peacefully and without glory. To the last minute, not the slightest doubt brushed his innocent soul. Yet, without knowing it, the final inheritor of the Umbrian tradition has won where the Adversary himself would have lost. Because if Nivasio Dolcemare has renounced the path which leads through a thousand adversities to eternal joy, that renunciation is due in large measure to the apotheosis of St. Dionysius the Areopagite, painted in the apse of the Catholic church in Athens by Ermengildo Buonfiglioli.

III.

One day Nivasio Dolcemare discovered that there was something hidden in the Greek Church, something that *must not be seen*. No one told Nivasio what it was, and Nivasio himself did not ask. Whom could he have asked? Frau Linda was absent-minded, moody, and did not like to speak of "certain things." Besides, Nivasio sensed that Frau Linda belonged to a different, hostile world. Still less could he ask his parents. It would have been like admitting a betrayal. Like telling his father and mother that he had gone over to the enemy. The rivalry between the Greek Church and the French Church was extremely fierce. It became even fiercer during Orthodox Holy Week. In the night after Holy Friday, when the image of the dead Christ is carried amid smoking torches, and the Greeks put candles in their windows, Casa Dolcemare remained as dark as if it were uninhabited.

A spectator of this rivalry, Nivasio himself remained neutral. Destiny predisposed him to overcome the defects of his family, his caste, his race. And not only the defects, but the merits as well. He foresaw that he would someday reach this form of supreme freedom. He was already modeling himself on the image of the Hard and Solitary Man, the Man of Diamond, a fusion of Achilles and Orlando, the walking Man of Stone.

Later he pondered:

"Whence comes this essentially solitary and disdainful form of pedagogy, which scorns wheezing sincerity and to direct action prefers cool deception and biting hypocrisy; whence if not from our nostalgia for the Man of Stone, from the desire that as many men as possible might be fortified into Men of Stone, from the hope that the Man of Flesh, the Marsupial Man, the Incurable Plebeian might some day vanish from the face of the earth?"

The night after Holy Friday led to the day of Resurrection. And when the announcement came that Christ was risen, and the bells all went off at once, the neighborhood children used to bombard Casa Dolcemare, and the habitation of the Skilofranki, the house of the French Dogs, with firecrackers.

From his window, Nivasio recognized the bombardiers as his playmates, but he was not surprised. He already sensed that even before the defects and merits, a man of superior destiny must overcome the "specifics" of his family, his place, his race: the "picturesque details" of life. And that such an "overcoming" is borne out in the manner of speech, the tone, the cadence, the accent. Because the superior man speaks a colorless, transparent, blank language. Even the shadow of an accent has vanished from this priestly, atonic tongue, stripped of all earthly allure. And thus we, accentless men, cultivate a nostalgia for accents, and seek in others this flavor and aroma which we no longer possess, believing that they know a pleasure that is denied to us. We grow sad at the call of "local voices," the "voices of things," the voices of men who are like things, who live like things, who suffer as things suffer: fishermen, ballerinas, manual workers. . . .

Antoine Calaroni came from the south, General Papatrapatakos from the north: they met in front of the theater billboard.

"Have you seen, Your Excellency?" asked Calaroni, pointing to the newly pasted-up poster. "Eleonora Duse is coming."

"Yes, yes," said the General. "The cares of command give me no respite night or day, but, just between us, I don't mind having a laugh every once in a while."

"But Duse," objected Calaroni, "is a tragedienne, a great tragedienne."

"Everyone knows that!" boomed the General, coughing authoritatively.

They bowed to each other without smiling. Antoine continued on his way northward, his legs collapsing under him like the springs of a worn-out divan. His Excellency attempted to go southward, but could not. He was deeply mortified. The humiliations that his artistic and literary ignorance had caused him were beyond number (when the Generaless was present, Papatrapatakos almost always managed to save the situation), but he had never been burned so badly as in this little confrontation with Calaroni. The General was not only mortified, he was infuriated. Who was this Eleonora Duse anyway, that a commander of armies should be ashamed if he has never heard of her? From the depths of his jingling, sparkling breast, General Papatrapatakos sent the "great tragedienne" a thousand curses.

In order to get into the Greek Church and find the "thing" that was hidden there, Nivasio had to keep trying new stratagems. He was not attracted by the Metropoli or the other big churches of the capital, but by a small country church, a chapel, a *paraclissio* located beyond the Upper Patissia.

Crows were flying in twos high in the sky. At the bottom of the ravine gleamed an ass's skull and a few bleached bones. Nivasio went into the Greek Church. Sometimes Frau Linda accompanied him. But before those stiff, emaciated saints, before that enormous eye enclosed in a golden triangle, the governess would say disdainfully, "Pah! What paintings! God is all psyche. He doesn't want portraits!"

Discipline kept Nivasio from replying. But how gladly he would have shouted at Frau Linda that she had no right to enter this church, that her place if anywhere was in the *gynaikon,* the area reserved for women, where she and her kind could be herded together like sheep.

The misogyny of the Greek Church was one of the chief reasons that Nivasio preferred the Greek Church to the other Churches. A church is a spiritual workshop. But how can one rise to the spiritual with women present? It was better when Frau Linda stayed outside, pulling the petals from daisies, picking camomile, or hunting for chicory.

Nivasio went in. He was happy, and at the same time troubled. This church was not "his" church. His act was rash and reprehensible.

A thin ray of light fell from the double slits of the windows. The Triangular Eye could not have stood any stronger light. The solitude of the Pantocrator weighed heavily in the thick smell of cold incense.

That day Frau Linda stayed outside. The presence of a woman would have stained the purity of such leaden monotheism. The gold web of the iconostasis gleamed in the half-light. From their metal cases, goat-faced saints with lunatic eyes stared into space. In the middle of the iconostasis was an arched opening masked by a curtain of red percale. Behind was the *hieron*.

Nivasio approached on tiptoe and stood listening. He heard labored breathing, the heavy sigh of Him who was hidden behind the inviolable partition.

The most tender compassion[9] came over Nivasio. Not the compassion inspired by a sick baby, a crying baby, a mistreated woman, but the far more profound compassion inspired by a man of forty who has not found his place in life and sits hopelessly among the cold ashes.

Nivasio *knew* that there, two steps away, behind the curtain of red percale, in the cold and inviolable chamber, on a chair losing its stuffing, wrapped in an overcoat turned green from wear, with a salt-and-pepper beard, his triangular eye half-hidden under a moth-eaten top-hat, weary and discouraged, sat the Greek God. And tears of warm pity welled up in his eyes.

He searched his mind for some way to bring a little comfort to the Theos, the Panteleimon, the Alphomega, the Triangular Eye, the solitary God, the friendless God, the shivering God. He went over all the "good" things he had had to eat, and now would like to share with the needy God: the rabbit stew that Nicolá prepared so well, the strudels, the poached fish, the Mavrodaphne wine. He would have liked to bring

Him some of the cigarettes his father had specially made with "beard of the Sultan" tobacco, and thought of adding a couple of Havana cigars from the big box that Etem Pasha had presented to his father, and that his father, who did not smoke cigars, kept in the bottom of the credenza. But how could he take so much without being noticed by his papa and mama?

When Nivasio came out of the church of the Greek God, the sun was setting. The governess's bright-colored dress moved through fields already strewn with shadow. Frau Linda had gathered a whole kerchief full of camomile.

"Tonight will be the night," Nivasio promised himself. And he returned home burdened with thoughts.

The endeavor to bring food and comfort to the Greek God was carried out much more easily than Nivasio had imagined. When Frau Linda's breathing became calm and regular, Nivasio quietly got out of bed, dressed quickly, and went downstairs carrying his shoes in his hand.

The house had that sepulchral "clamminess" given off by sleeping people. Among the chief obstacles which in Nivasio's mind might have blocked his nocturnal endeavor was the darkness of the night and the impossibility of turning on a light. But as he came down the stairs, he saw with amazement that the house was full of light. He was about to turn back when he noticed that the light was empty and uninhabited. The light of the moon came in the wide-open windows and spread through the rooms, passing between the long shadows of the furniture. And the furniture led its own quiet life, breathing peacefully, savoring a wise, silent, barely perceptible joy, which no one in the daytime would have noticed.

This diffuse luminosity, this peaceful, polar brightness spread over the inertia of night, increased the solemnity of the nocturnal adventure. Nivasio felt happy, secure. The moonlight not only favored his plans, it also filled him with limitless confidence.

"Why doesn't life always go on in this light?" Nivasio wondered. In this calm and steady light, Nivasio Dolcemare found a certain changelessness, a durability that the light of the sun did not have.

The precaution he had taken of slipping little bits of wood into the latch of the credenza and the keyhole of the pantry door proved highly useful. Nivasio took some food from the credenza, brought a bottle of sweet wine from the pantry, and put everything into the straw basket that Frau Linda used to take on picnics to the country, which had the words *Frohes Wandern*[10] written diagonally across it in red wool. He added some cigarettes and two cigars from Etem Pasha's box, and went out of the house, closing the door very gently behind him until it touched the wooden block placed against the doorjamb, by means of which Nivasio ensured his re-entry.

For weapons, Nivasio took his father's sword-cane and a long bread knife which he slipped into his belt. A window-blind creaked on the second floor, but the sound was followed by silence, and after waiting a long moment with bated breath, Nivasio stepped away from the wall as if he were setting out to walk on water.

The road was straight and bright. Not a soul was to be seen. Nivasio passed the Papanastassopoulos's garden. Behind the gates, the lawn chairs arranged in a family circle continued on their own the conversation that had gone on during the day between the Papanastassopouloses and their guests. The playthings of little Fulli, Luluca's baby brother, were scattered over the moonlit gravel: a rocking horse, a rubber ball, a toy cannon.

"*My* Luluca," thought Nivasio, looking up at her room on the second floor. But suddenly he froze: there was light in her window.

His first impulse was to call out to Luluca. The thought of being seen by Luluca, alone, in the street, at that extraordinary hour, excited him; still more the hope that Luluca would come down and go with him on his bold adventure.

Nivasio drew his breath to whistle, but the fear that instead of Luluca, Mrs. Peterson might come to the window, stopped him. Then a new thought canceled his previous thoughts.

"Luluca is my friend," thought Nivasio. "My only friend. She will always be my friend. But Luluca is a woman. And in certain things no woman, not even Luluca, can participate. Heroic undertakings, daring deeds, must be carried out by men alone. Otherwise they lose their value."

Nivasio looked up at the window. He was torn between the voice of duty and the voice of his heart.

"Alone," he repeated to himself. And at the same moment, he noticed that the light in the window was only moonlight reflected on the glass.

The chill of disillusion extinguished his illusions. Nothing remained of the plans he had devised; all that was left was the idea of Luluca sleeping. Nivasio felt the weight, the hostility of that sleep hanging over him.[11]

"I am alone in the night," thought Nivasio Dolcemare, "I am setting out on a desperate adventure, and you sleep!" He was on the point of crying out Luluca's name, of driving his cry into the heart of that sleep. But he changed his mind. Banging the iron tip of the cane on the pavement, he went down the deserted road, disappointed but pure.

He had just passed the gymnasium of the "Herakleion" health club when he noticed a green light moving ahead of him on the road, apparently the taillight of an out-of-service tram. He could not see the horses, but he could hear the metallic rumble of the carriage, the creaking of the wheels, the clank of the chains, the "hups" and "ha's" of the driver urging his beasts on. He was surprised that a tram could have passed by without his noticing it, but while he was searching for an explanation of this mystery, the tram turned off in the direction of the Evelpidi military school, and its metallic rumble was gradually swallowed by the night.

After the unexpected appearance of this living "thing," the solitude weighed more heavily, and when even the last sonorous trace of the mysterious tram was submerged in the deepest silence, Nivasio slashed the air three times with the point of his cane, not so much, as he thought, to test the release of the spring and the flourish of the blade, as to give himself courage. Three times the triangular stiletto leaped out with a brief flash and stood firm on its hilt like a bayonet on the barrel of a rifle.

The houses gradually thinned out. They were separated by dense gardens and uncultivated fields. Athens is not surrounded by an industrial zone, bare walls, schematic structures, black canals full of greasy water, but passes without transition from city to country. These "last" houses were villas gleaming in the midst of their grounds, little palaces shining among the trees.

By its slender tower topped with a cone of slate in which the moon was reflected, Nivasio recognized the villa of Mavromicali, the millionaire beggar who left his house every morning at dawn carrying a little hooked stick and went around hunting for cigar butts. At the moment, Nivasio did not think about the millionaire's strange habits, but it occurred to him—who knows why?—that Mavromicali means "Michael the Black."

He came to Clonaridi. The moon shone on the windows of the brewery. Folded chairs rested two by two against little iron tables on the public terrace. A cat crossed the street like a shadow.

Apart from the brewery, there was only the Antirabies Institute, which was a small, square building with studded walls, sitting on top of an embankment and approachable only by an entrenched stairway. Nivasio had never seen the windows of the Antirabies Institute open; no sound had ever issued from inside those walls; yet he knew that within that house men transformed into dogs were kept in iron cages, baying horribly and tearing at their hands with slavering jaws.

Nivasio heard someone call him. He wheeled around: there was no one there. But someone might have been hiding in the sunken stairway. Nivasio began to run, pointing his cane in front of him with the dagger gleaming at its tip.

The city street narrowed to a country road, then to a path, then the path disappeared. Nivasio stopped with his heart in his throat.

The crows that flew in twos high in the sky during the day could not be seen in the darkness of night, but there must have been many of them, because their croaking filled the air. The bleached bones of asses marked out a white road that crossed the valley and dropped below the dark horizon. To the left, a little cube sitting in a field and extended by its shadow, appeared the *paraclissio* of the Greek God.

Only then did it occur to Nivasio that his efforts might be in vain. The door of the *paraclissio* was probably locked at that hour.

Nivasio approached the church, crossed the porch, and tried the latch.

The door was open.

Nivasio went in. The church was dark, but from behind the partition of the iconostasis came a weak, wavering yellow light through which from time to time a thin column of blue smoke rose and scattered.

Nivasio quickly grasped the situation. The Greek God was sitting behind the percale curtain, by candle-light, smoking a cigarette.

Nivasio approached the hieron. He heard a low mumbling. Someone was praying. Who else could be praying at that hour, in that lonely church, if not the Greek God? And who else could the Greek God be praying to, if not himself? At first the idea of a God praying to himself troubled Nivasio's mind. Then the logic of such prayer became clear to him. This prayer of a God who believes in himself is prayer par excellence, the prayer of prayers. Nivasio moved closer.

But the closer he came to the hieron, the more uncertain he grew whether God should be addressed as "Lord" or in some other way. Finally the word *Kyrie* came spontaneously to his lips, and he repeated it twice aloud: *"Kyrie! Kyrie!"*

No one answered. In fact it seemed to Nivasio that after his cry, even the mumbled praying stopped. Nivasio drew closer still, bent down, pushed the basket of provisions under the curtain, but suddenly he screamed: his wrist was seized in an iron grip.

"No! No!" Nivasio began to shout. "Let me go! I didn't do anything wrong! I just wanted to bring you a few things. They are good things. Look. . . ."

To the terror aroused by the touch of that hand was added the far greater terror of the imminent appearance of Him whom it is death to see.

"Let me go!" Nivasio kept shouting. "They are good things, from our house. . . ."

The curtain opened. The hand that clutched his appeared, and behind that hand "He" stood, enormous, in a white nightshirt, his face beardless and swollen, his head bristling with little demons.

"No!" cried Nivasio again, his eyes dazzled by the unexpected sight.

A heavy silence fell. Then Frau Linda, standing tall in the moonlight, said:

"Tomorrow, we shall have to take some purgative: *ein wenig Ricinusoel.*"

IV.

The same moon that had aided Nivasio Dolcemare in his nocturnal attempt to discover the Greek God, also lent its brightness to a ritual of the purest poetry.

At the summit of the Acropolis, before a few privileged guests, Eleonora Duse, standing on the steps of the Parthenon, hieratic in the white gown of Anna, recited a passage from *La Città Morta.*

"Do you not think, Bianca Maria, that the statues on fountains must be happy? In their immobile and enduring beauty flows a living spirit that is ever renewed. . . ."

Leaning against a section of fallen column, his head resting on the back of his hand, Antoine Calaroni listened.

"They partake at once of stillness and fluidity."

At that point there was a small explosion and a little flame flared up among the illustrious ruins. A prolonged "ssh" ran through the audience, a whisper of indignation rose from the sacred precinct. Crumpled in shame, General Papatrapatakos blew out the flame and hid his cigarette under his kepi. Eleonora Duse went on:

"In solitary gardens they sometimes seem like exiles, yet they are not, for their fluid souls are forever in touch with the far-off mountains. . . ."

No applause followed the final phrase as it soared moonwards, but a noble shudder ran through the audience.

The Duke of A. took the Great Lady's arm, and they went slowly down the steps of the Propylaea. The rest followed, brothers in the cult of poetry.

The next day, Antoine Calaroni met General Papatrapatakos, who asked him for his impressions. Calaroni raised to heaven the two oyster-like molluscs that served him as eyes, pressed his right hand to his heart, and exlaimed:

"Bublime! Unborbettable!"

His Excellency did not bat an eye, but for the first time in his life he doubted his own intelligence.

The "dream solution" did not put an end to Nivasio Dolcemare's love for the unapproachable Greek God. On the contrary. But with the difference that after the "dream solution," Nivasio was more convinced than ever that he was personally forbidden to see the Forty-year-old God hidden behind the gilded web of the iconostasis in the *paraclissio* of the Upper Patissia.

This prohibition grieved him. But if he was not permitted to see the Greek God standing behind the curtain of the inviolable sanctuary, there always remained the slim chance of meeting him in the street, in a café, or on a tram.

In hopes of one day coming across Him for whom he had faced the human and more-than-human dangers of the night, Nivasio began to peer closely into the faces of people he met in the street, especially when they had grizzled beards and a look of near starvation.

One day Nivasio went shopping with Signora Trigliona. It was a March afternoon, already troubled by the approach of spring. The shops swarmed with people crowding around the counters like flies on warm excrement. The smell of the fabrics, the milky pallor of the clerks, the abrupt way they slashed at pieces of silk, filled Nivasio with horror. He put up with it all in hopes of the fateful meeting.

Cross-hatched by the zig-zag flight of bats, the evening sky looked like an emerald mirror at which a giant had hurled a large stone. The shops in Hermes Street were lit up like theaters. Signora Trigliona stood staring into the window of Abastado Brothers with unusual constancy for so flighty a woman. In the thoughtless head of Signora Trigliona, under a wide Florentine straw hat covered with cherries, the last doubts were being dispelled. That magnificent piece of Venetian lace, displayed in honor on a black velvet cushion which emphasized its arachnean delicacy, was the very piece that Countess Pantera, Visanio's mother, had given her as a wedding present. Who had dared to violate the "secret compartment" of the linen chest, where the precious lace was hidden along with other family treasures?

The gallop of two exhausted horses took Signora Trigliona back home. She flew to the second floor like a montgolfier caught in a hurricane. She opened the chest: the secret compartment was empty.

The same horses carried Signora Trigliona to the Director of Urban Legal Services. Colonel Tsé received her immediately and placed beneath her the finest chair in his office.

"Signogha," the Colonel began, "I have long awaited this moment. . . . I have long . . ."

"Colonel," exclaimed Signora Trigliona, collapsing into the chair, "I am ruined!"

Colonel Tsé's mind clouded. Albeit a certain ideal cloudedness, if one may put it so, was the Colonel's normal mental condition. Instinctively, he imitated the tone of his lady visitor.

"Ghuined?"

"Ruined!" repeated Signora Trigliona with tragic passion. Colonel Tsé's thoughts cleared. This suffering was a woman's wile, a simulated modesty. Tsé pulled at his cuffs and made a foray.

"The Commendatoghe?"

Signora Trigliona leaped to her feet.

"Please! My husband knows nothing!"

Tsé was no longer in any doubt. He relaxed, became gallant.

"Have no fear, Signogha. . . ."

"But you don't understand, Colonel! His mother gave me that lace, and her mother gave it to her. . . ."

"Whose mother . . . ? What ouace. . . ?"

"You have seen it on me many times, Colonel. My antique Venetian lace. . . ."

"What about it?"

"Stolen!"

"Damn!"

Colonel Tsé stepped back. His exclamation had nothing to do with the stolen lace. The man had to yield once again to the police chief. Tsé went behind his desk and sat down with a professional air.

"Let us pghoceed in an oghderly fashion, Signogha. You were saying?"

While, in the office smelling of creolin, Signora Trigliona told the Director of Urban Legal Services what had happened, Nivasio, left waiting in the anteroom, listened as some policemen explained to him the workings of the Gras rifle.

Though Nivasio, as Giambattista Vico says in his *Book of Elements,* was destined by nature "to live in Plato's republic, not to mingle with Romulus's crowd," the mystery of firearms held an irresistible fascination for him, as for all men of healthy verility. For Antoine Calaroni, as we have said, firearms were mute objects. But however fascinating the mechanics of the Gras rifle, Nivasio could not take his eyes off of a certain grey-haired, weary-looking man who came through the lobby dragging his feet and went to hang his whip on a hook.

Feeling himself stared at, the grey-haired man came over to Nivasio.

"Do I displease the young gentleman?"

"No . . . sir. . . ," Nivasio mumbled, melting with shame.

The presumed God (it was Anastasios the dog-catcher, who hated little boys because they always pelted him with stones while he was performing his duties) reached his hand out and brushed the "young gentleman's" nose with his finger.

"Disgusting!" he muttered, and shuffled off like a bear.

Signora Trigliona was upset. As she went out the door, she picked Nivasio up as one picks up a coat thrown over a chair.

"Home," she said to the coachman, "but don't gallop." The coachman set the horses at a trot.

The ambiguous nature of the interview, the suspicion that Hermione, her faithful chambermaid, was connected with the gang of Cosma the Leaper, the insinuations of "that stupid Tsé," his ridiculous attempts to turn an official visit into an amorous assignation, left Signora Trigliona deeply disturbed.

"Don't tell anyone where we went today," she cautioned the coachman before getting out of the carriage, and this reliance on the complicity of a servant disturbed her mind most of all.

She called for Hermione to come and undress her. "I want to see her face," she thought. She was anxious to see the chambermaid with her "new" face of an accomplice of Cosma the Leaper. She prepared herself for this "ploy," this "great deception," this "impassibility that betrays no suspicion." If someone had told her at that moment that the theft of the lace had given her one of the greatest pleasures of her life, Signora Trigliona would have protested vehemently. But in truth Signora Trigliona had never felt before such a deep, full, 'shivering' voluptuousness, not even when she found herself for the first time naked in the arms of Commendatore Visanio.

Hermione came in. Between the high-necked black dress and the white crest poised on the modest arrangement of her hair, the face of the chambermaid was all purity, honesty, candor. "What an impostor!" thought her victim, studying the maid's face in the indirect light of the mirror—a trick she had learned from the detective novels of Gaboriau. And at the touch of that delicate hand, that hand trained to rob, perhaps even to kill, Signora Trigliona felt the most exquisite tremors run down her spine.

Commendatore Visanio was away.

Signora Trigliona did not close her eyes all night. When she thought everyone was asleep, she armed herself with a brass poker from the fireplace and went to inspect the locks and bolts. With every breath of wind, she ran to the window and peered out into the garden. She listened to the whispering of the trees, the small voices of night, the round call of the hoopoe. She watched the moon go down. She beheld the radiant dawn. She heard the universal chorus of birds greet the morning. Her heart throbbed. In the air of that unusual hour there was a certain balladic freshness. At eight o'clock, the horse of the chief of police rode up to the gate.

She went down to open the door herself, and led the Colonel to the scene of the crime. Her precautions, however justified, underscored the ambiguous nature of the situation. Tsé walked inspiredly in the wake of that frothy, perfumed dressing gown. In a tight-fitting checkered jacket, his riding crop tucked into a tawny boot, his buttocks protected by a leather heart, dry and sinewy, the old Colonel was an impeccable example of the remains of a lady-killer.

Having made his inspection, which was fruitless in any case, the Colonel said, "And now, Signogha, I would ouike to see *her*."

Signora Trigliona placed her pink hand on the bell-pull. Pelopidas appeared in the doorway.

"A cup of coffee for the Colonel, Pelopidas. Tell Hermione to bring it."

Hermione came in with the tray. A mere schoolgirl. The Colonel approached her, bending down like Narcissus.

"What is your name, my beauty?"

"With my lady's permission?"

"Of course, Hermione."

"My name is Hermione, sir."

"Heghmione! Hm! Hm!"

The Colonel cleared his throat and drew himself up.

"Tell me, Heghmione, just between us: do you know Cosma the Oueaper?"

The chambermaid's eyes snapped open like the lens of a camera. Tray and cup crashed to the floor, and Hermione sprang to the windowsill. The Colonel and Signora Trigliona rushed in that direction, but the window was already empty. And when they looked out, horrified, expecting to see the girl's broken body on the ground below, Hermione was already running off through the flowerbeds.

"Stop or I'll shoot!" the Colonel ordered, pointing his bare hand at the fleeing girl with his index finger extended.

Standing on top of the garden wall, Hermione looked back at him with an angelic smile. On the other side was the flourishing garden of the Peristeri's. Hermione waved good-bye and plunged into the greenery like a swimmer jumping into the sea.

"Good Loghd!" exclaimed the Colonel. As the skirt billowed in mid-air, there appeared from under it a pair of socks, a pair of garters, a pair of muscular calves.

"A man!" cried Signora Trigliona.

"Cosma the Oueaper," murmured Colonel Tsé.

The tune of "La Gran Via" rang out mysteriously in the air. It was followed by an astonished silence. Then an auroral light spread over Signora Trigliona's cheeks.

"My god!" she whispered, covering her face with her hands. "How many times has he seen me naked?"

The Colonel had just time to catch the perfumed weight on his chest. He shook his fist at the trees in Peristeri's garden.

"Scoundghel!" he hissed through his tinted moustache. "For this one insult alone, I will take you, I will cghush you like a woghm!"

The next day, Signora Trigliona, accompanied by Nivasio, betook herself to the Saranti Agency. It was located on Aeolus Street, next to the octagonal tower dedicated to the God of Winds.

When the door of the Saranti Agency was opened, it caused a little bell to ring: *ding!* The Saranti Agency occupied a single room which was divided into sections by means of green cotton curtains which slid on metal rods.

At the sound of the little bell which announced the entrance of Signora Trigliona and Nivasio into the employment agency, the righthand curtain contracted before the melancholy face of Signor Saranti. He nodded in recognition of his visitor and made a broad welcoming gesture.

"Madame Dolcemare, my respects."

There was a little thud. Nivasio had fainted. Saranti and Signora Trigliona carried him behind the curtain, laid him down on a straw divan, and sprinkled his face with water.

"He is in a stage of development," said Signor Saranti in a smoke-hoarsened voice.

"He didn't eat any breakfast," said Signora Trigliona.

Brought back to his senses and assailed with questions, Nivasio stared wide-eyed at Signor Saranti, shut his eyes again with a shudder, and from the darkness behind his eyelids murmured, "I know nothing. . . , I know nothing. . . ."

Commendatore Visanio was a man of authority. Doubt tormented him, uncertainty harrowed him, a plurality of choices offered him in any circumstances condemned him to perpetual inaction, but this all went on in the depths of his consciousness, in a place inaccessible to others, and into which no one except himself ever stuck his nose. As one clamps a lid over the stinking pit of a cesspool, so Commendatore Visanio clamped over the stinking pit of consciousness the lid of an imposing authority. "A society so organized that each person does what needs to be done," was for Commendatore Visanio a necessary illusion. Nivasio had fainted at the sight of Signor Saranti? A singular and mysterious fact. But in the face of such "dark" events, Commendatore Visanio beat a dignified retreat. Summoned urgently, Doctor Naso prescribed rest, a plain diet, and a tonic to be taken orally. Commendatore Visanio was back on familiar ground. He explained to Signora Trigliona that "orally" meant "through the mouth," and returned to the peace of mind of a man who knows that he has "done what needed to be done." And he thought no more about it. Thanks to the treatment prescribed by the proper authority, Nivasio would no longer faint at the sight of Signor Saranti.

For a long time, the Bolshevik authorities traveled around with a false Lenin, while the true Lenin, precious and vulnerable, stayed hidden in the depths of the Kremlin. Famous jewels sleep in the darkness of strongboxes, while their poor glass brothers enjoy themselves on the bare flesh of their owners. From Kâ to the Look-alike of Nikolai Ilych, the system of Doubles has been successfully practiced. Appearance is sovereign. Even the most inaccessible woman can be possessed in the skin of her double. But one point remains obscure. Had Nivasio indeed recognized in Signor Saranti the Forty-year-old God Himself, whom he had tried in vain to catch sight of in the *paraclissio* of the Upper Patissia, or, as with Lenin's followers and the amateurs of jewels, had he been satisfied with a convenient likeness, a simulacrum, a numen? Strange in any case was the coincidence between the supposed deity of the agent and his name, which in translation means "Mister Forty."

Signor Saranti was a famous agent, the greatest, the one and only agent of Athens. The Saranti Employment Agency might have been adorned with that title which the Germans express with the word *Hofflieferant,* meaning "Purveyor to the Royal Household," if the Royal Household of Greece had not had far more sure and effective means for recruiting its own personal staff. Apart from that, the Saranti Agency did not know the meaning of failure.

Signor Saranti was a profoundly serious, profoundly sad man. Sadness is the color of nobility. One of his clients once said of him, "Despite his occupation, he is an honest man." "Saranti is a respectable person," another added quickly. "Respectable?" thought Nivasio. "Signor Saranti is a God!"

But to call Signor Saranti a God is only half the truth. For Signor Saranti was not just a God, but a Greek God. The Greek God is less an Abstract Entity than a Demiurge, that is, a Working God, a Passionate God, a God subject to hunger, anger, cold, and to the sky-blue happiness inspired by children's games; a God who leaves the deep mark of his shoes behind him when he walks; a God who, wherever he rests his hand, leaves an imprint in the form of a fig leaf; a God who, when he breathes, warms the air and revives the greenery.

And yet among Demiurges, Signor Saranti was the least of Demiurges, the lowest in authority, the most down-at-heel. His power extended only to the Employment Agency next to the octagonal tower dedicated to the God of Winds, where he ruled over three little sections: of women, men, and *groomi.* According to the client's wishes, he would draw the green curtain, uncovering one of the three sections, and present the creatures created by his hairy, nicotine-yellowed hands. A woman? At a gesture from the Demiurge, Signor Saranti's female creations would rise simultaneously from their bench against the wall: thin or fat, busty or breastless, bearded or glabrous, whole or fragmentary; but all equally inert, mute, blank-faced, lifeless, stamped from clay.

At a sign from the Demiurge, the chosen one[12] would separate herself from the original group, take three steps forward, and become animate: the Demiurge's sign had brought her to life. A glimmer of individuality emerged from that clay already colored by the crude, torpid soul of the slave. The arm rose at an angle, the mouth spread into a joyless smile, the eyes began to roll, the creature was alive, spoke, presented herself. She was ready to go, to join the realm of her new owner. The regular, automatic, repeated gestures of daily housework already stirred her limbs: sweeping, making the beds, cooking, washing dishes, stuffing her mistress's breasts into their corset, proffering her behind for the master's pinches, initiating the young master into the joys of sex, stealing. And while the miracle of creation took place, "La Valse de la Poupèe," slowed to the tempo of a funeral march, played softly, mysteriously through the Employment agency.

I can come into a room,
Bow this way and that way,
Curtsy, greet the guests.
I can dance the gavotte
But my minuet is best.

Don't you like my little step?
In the waltz they find me charming
And deliciously disarming.
La la la
I am Alexia!

In the intervals between one creation and the next, a subdued murmur came from behind the closed curtains and spread through the Agency. It was the primordial language of creatures as yet excluded from life, the twittering of birds stamped from clay, the sound of stilt-legged tantali speaking from the depths of the Eocene.

The little bell rings: *ding!* This time the client is looking for a male. A male!

At a gesture from the Demiurge, the curtain opens upon those destined for slavery. Ten masks, ten mannequins, ten shooting gallery figures. Faces poised above white paper collars, bow-ties painted on their shirtfronts, major-domo's epaulettes cut from dried corn silk. Rubber biceps, moving oddly under the sleeves of the zebra-striped jackets, suggest the muscles of a valet who will successfully replace his cachetic master in his mistress's bed. A chorus of low and extremely distant voices accompanies the exhibition of these not yet alive but already domesticated creatures.

My lord,
Your glass.
My lady,
It's time for Mass.

A third ring of the bell: *ding!* The client this time is a bachelor. The Demiurge draws the third curtain aside, revealing a joyous array of *groomi*. For convenience of terminology, the Demiurge has simply given a local ending to the English word "groom." There stand ten sexless creatures, who reproduce by autogenesis like single-celled molluscs. Dressed in the scarlet uniforms of petty demons. Tail-coat split up to the middle of the back. A row of gold buttons ending in a tadpole tail. Puffy cheeks, big glassy eyes, heart-shaped little mouths, pie-pan hats slanted across their varnished hair, pudgy hands hanging by the seams of their trousers, unsuited to any manly labors.

The client gazes with shining eyes. At a sign from the Demiurge, the *groomi* all turn around. The client's perplexity increases. During the difficult time of decision, a chorus of *castrati* sings:

Pómila pómila pómila po
Pómila pómila pómila po.
Anixi portélo
Gamissi pinélo
Ton écho megálo
Egó ghia sé.
Pómila pómila pómila po
Pómila pómila pómila po.[13]

The choice is made. The chorus stops. There is a gleam of laughter from the divine Hermaphroditus.

V.

The Saranti Establishment had no competitors. . . . Or, rather, had only one: a woman. Who else but a woman would have dared rival a Demiurge? Her name was Basilica, which means "the queenly one."

Basilica functioned less as an employment agent than as a protector of young girls. Basilica had no fixed place of business, like Signor Saranti's office, but moved about in the open air. In good weather, Basilica occupied a bench in the Royal Palace Square, the third from the left as you entered from Constitution Square.

Basilica was abundant, expansive, loud. Her backside entirely filled a seat intended for four people. Cybele in her chariot was not so majestic as Basilica on her bench in Royal Palace Square. She sat with her legs spread, her elbows on her knees, her palms open, ready to take to her ample bosom all the homeless girls, runaways, rejects, fugitives, truants, all the wild, anarchic, delinquent, or betrayed girls who converged on her unofficial bench from the four corners of the city.

More than a dispenser of work, Basilica was a spiritual guide, a counselor, a mama for these stray girls. And occasionally, amid all this tattered flesh, she would come upon some "unspoiled" country girl, some peasant lass, some little flower of the field. These were Basilica's "great finds." On such occasions, she would hire Thrasyboulos Cacatea's landau.

With the flare of a festive coupé, windows down, trim gleaming, wood shining, yellow wheels pin-striped in black, the landau of Thrasyboulos Cacatea was drawn by a pair of bay horses with enormous rumps and crisp manes, tassled and garlanded with little bells. As for Thrasyboulos himself, the owner and driver of this magnificent rig, he sat up on his box in bottle-green livery with gold buttons, a silk hat with a cockade on his head and a beribboned whip in his hand.

When Basilica went for one of her "drives," it was an event. Squeezed into one corner of the landau, the feather on her head nodding in pace with the big horses, face powdered, discs of rouge on her cheeks, turnip hands folded on her still inviolate lap, nose buried in the feathers of a little boa like a pullet hunting for fleas, the latest pupil sat to the left of Basilica, who, herself plumed and flowered, wrapped in a feathery anaconda, her lard squeezed into silk, her breasts pushed up to her chin, her face shining like a ripe tomato, enormous and oscillating, filled the rest of the carriage, giving it a distinct list to starboard.

At intersections, in front of cafés, the *gameádes,*[14] the epicures, the fanciers of fresh meat, fifty-year-old plethorics with their epigastra stuffed into piqué waistcoats, their moustaches waxed with shoe-polish, their jowls close-shaven and blue, their homburgs pushed over one ear, winked their eyes and elbowed each other as the landau drove by.

"Did you see the 'new' one?"

"Nice stuff!"

"Aklaston kreas."[15]

And the landau passed with a jingle of little bells.

An enormous Red Hand hung at the end of Stadium Street, wrist up and fingers pointing to the sidewalk.

The Red Hand was the sign of the Biruni Sisters, Glovers. But in exceptional cases it would raise itself miraculously, close into a fist, and point a stiff index finger in the direction of danger. The Biruni Sisters sold gloves, but everyone knew that the Biruni Sisters were really three sirens in disguise, who performed flying copulations, quick erotic tricks, and lucrative aphrodisms in the back of their shop. No serious citizen would ever go into the Biruni Sisters' shop to be fitted with gloves. Informed sources said that the sign of the Red Hand itself concealed an immodest symbol; but who puts much faith in the language of symbols?

Thrasyboulos Cacatea's landau has just passed by; the tinkle of its little bells was just fading into the noises of the street, when above the heads of the three *gameádes* who had stopped in front of the Biruni Sisters' shop and were still heatedly discussing the latest "novelty" being driven around by Basilica, there burst out a horrendous shriek of rusty metal and the miracle of the Red Hand occurred. People fled in all directions. First to flee were the three *gameádes,* who put such ardor into the race that their heels kicked the backs of their heads.

Preceded by a golden hum, by the arcane voice of

the miracle, the Carriage of the Future made its first appearance in the city of Pericles.

The truncated phaeton glided along noiselessly. It was shiny, black, high-sprung. The nonchalant driver sat in front. He manipulated the tiller with a gloved hand. He was bold and impassive. He had blue eyes, blond whiskers, and a visored cap. Behind him sat the Lady. The Lady of Ladies. Bunches of fat grapes hung from her towering coiffure, and wood grouse fluttered in it. Her globose breasts swelled the lace on her bodice to the calm rhythm of her breathing. Her swan's neck, caught tightly in a pillory of mountain-lace, rose high above her leg-of-mutton sleeves. Balanced in the point-lace of her gloved hand, the fringe of her parasol poured over the folded top like the leaves of a weeping willow. The Lady's face was enamel, her eyes crystal, her smile coral. Which face, eyes, and smile she turned now right, now left, greeting the empty street, the crowd that was not there, like a queen without subjects, the Empress of the Void.

Basilica lived at the foot of the Likavettos, in a little dovecot, a fairy cottage. It was a mystery how all of her could fit into it.

The night after the "drive," the most impatient of the *gameádes* would hasten down the slope of the Likavettos and knock at the fairy's cottage: "Tap! Tap!"

A window would open.

"Who's there?"

"Kokonaki, the grocer. Was that a relative of yours I saw with you in Thrasyboulos Cacatea's landau?"

"My niece, yes. Why do you ask?"

"We wondered if we could spend a little time with her. . . ."

"Shame on you, Mister Kokonaki! Titika is still just as her dear mother made her. She's a child, a flower of the field."

"We don't mean her any harm, Basilica. Who do you take us for?"

They would hear the slap of slippers on the stairs.

The door would open, and the *gameádes* would slip in sideways, like crabs.

"Don't wake her up on me, for pity's sake! She's a child, a little flower. . . ."

The subsequent appearances of the Carriage of the Future gradually dispelled the astonishment of its first appearance. People peered out through their blinds; then they risked going down to the street; finally they began walking around again without fear.

The automobile had come by sea, from the rich and distant West. It went about silently,[16] avoided steep descents, and in the face of steep ascents dignifiedly took the long way round. It preferred the aristocratic to the popular quarters. It was pursued by a train of agile, barefoot *páides,* who, when circumstances permitted, would break its headlamps with stones.

The appearance of the automobile caused great astonishment, but in terms of form it was sharply criticized. More than once, Nivasio Dolcemare heard the automobile compared to a decapitated body. Cries of alarm were raised over the threatened beauty of the carriage team. Committees of defense were organized for the protection of the coach-and-four.

The conservatives would say: "That it is practical, I grant you. But beautiful? No!"

To which the progressives would reply: "Beauty is a convention. What is not beautiful today will be beautiful tomorrow."

These disputes inflamed the city, disturbed the peace of families, set sons against fathers.

Nivasio seemed to sympathize with the progressives, since they were in the minority, but at bottom he was unable to take either side. From the dim depths of childhood, the "problems" of serious people had always inspired in him the greatest distrust. For lack of judgment, instinct told him that these apparently contrary opinions were in effect two different aspects of the same form of stupidity.

And what new miracles does progress have in store for us? With what new beauties will Immortal Idiocy adorn herself?

Signor Forty was so diligent in his efforts to please his clients that he even managed to please the widow Trimis. Not that the widow was hard to please. She was meek, careful never to offend, timid as a prematurely aged gazelle. But the widow Trimis lived with her eighteen-year-old son Epaminondas and her brother-in-law Aristogeiton, a dental surgeon and an extremely lascivious man.

While poor Philopemon was alive, the Trimises spent many years in Paris. Epaminondas was born there and baptized in Ste.-Marie-des-Batignolles. The widow looked back on her life in Paris as a time of insuperable splendor. The furniture in the Trimis house—all of it "trick" furniture—stood as mute testimony to that distant age of gold.

No piece of furniture in the Trimis house corresponded to its own appearance. What looked like a bookcase was really an armoire. The armoire, in turn, was a vertical bed which could be transformed at need into a horizontal bed. When you pulled a drawer in the chest, the entire front opened, revealing a medicine cabinet for diathermic treatments, internally illuminated by a constellation of little blue lights. The cushions on the chairs concealed either a chamber pot, in the old fashion, or, in the more modern fashion, a musical bellows which under the sitter's weight emitted indecent crepitations. A glass full of liquor on the dining room table invited one to drink, but the ruby-colored liquid was actually solid and permanently glued to the bottom of the glass. A cloth canary slept in a golden cage. On a false cube of sugar, a false fly dropped a tiny, false fly-speck. A large, remarkably lifelike piece of excrement sat on the mantle in the drawing room.

The transporting of this furniture from Paris to Athens cost an arm and a leg, but how could one abandon such original, such "Parisian" furniture, much of which had been designed by Philopemon himself? In his family, he had enjoyed the reputation of an artist and an eccentric. As evidence, they would point to a little table he had made entirely from wooden spools strung on iron rods, a bust of his grandfather modeled in bread, the portrait of a deceased aunt composed from the dead woman's own hair.

Aristogeiton spent his mornings extirpating molars, canines, premolars, and incisors from those unfortunates who, seduced by the modest prices posted on his door, came trustingly into the dentist's office and left a short time later clutching their jaws and howling like dogs.

Aristogeiton had been practicing his violent surgery for years. His deltoid muscles swelled like the muscles of a weight lifter. These athletic exercises gave him an enormous appetite. Aristogeiton ate like a horse, digested like Polyphemus. Stuffed, unbuttoned, his bare feet stuck into embroidered slippers, he sat himself for his postprandial labors on the kitchen terrace, surveying through a pair of navy binoculars the serving girls of the neighborhood who, in that panic, solar hour, stood at their kitchen windows washing the dishes and singing of the joys and torments of love.

Every time one of these dishwashers came within his reach, the dentist mercilessly impregnated her.

The maintenance of maids in the Trimis household became an insoluble problem. The widow Trimis laid her case before Signor Forty, and he began sending her his coarsest, most repulsive women: a month later the poor things would be carrying one of Aristogeiton's creatures under their hearts. In despair, the widow appealed to Signor Forty.

"Your brother-in-law is quite a rabbit!" the agent exclaimed, pleased in his capacity as demiurge at such a display of fertility. "Leave it to me, I have just the right thing for you this time: a hunchback."

The widow was a bit dubious, but the hope of finding a maid who was proof against Aristogeiton's ardors overcame her superstitious fears.

The hunchback, who was not only hunchbacked but also bald, noseless, prognathous, one-eyed, and had a hare-lip, was named Aspasia. An era of peace and sterility dawned in the Trimis household.

One day the hideous maid was in the kitchen with her mistress. They were preparing together a dish made from eggplants and tomatoes, known as Imambaildi, at the mere taste of which, according to tradition, Mahomet had fainted from pleasure, when suddenly Aspasia herself nearly fainted.

"Sit down for a moment," said the widow Trimis. "What's the matter?"

Aspasia turned her one eye away guiltily.

"Aspasia, you are hiding something from me!"

"It's not my fault," the monster muttered between sobs, "it was the doctor. . . ."

After the scandal of Cosma the Leaper, Signor Forty sent two successive maids to Casa Dolcemare: both island girls, both highly recommended, both, as it turned out, dangerous criminals.

The first, Parigoria, which means Consolation, "ate" a black pearl pendant which Signora Trigliona had placed on the dressing table in her bedroom the night before, and then went to digest it in the house of her lover, a police commissioner in Colonel Tsé's jurisdiction. The second, Sebaste, meaning Worshipful, was so intolerant of reproaches that when Signora Trigliona criticized some detail of her service, she turned around, hoisted her skirts, and showed her backside. The Dolcemares were left once again without a maid.

The day on which Sebaste, after a scene even more violent than the preceding one,[17] was thrown out on the street by the stout arm of Pelopidas, who then threw her bundle of personal effects out the window, was a tragic day in Casa Dolcemare. A black cloud hung over everyone and everything. The unbearable tendency of "serious" people to dramatize the most trivial themes, lent itself once again to the critical meditations of Nivasio, who, silent and circumspect, followed the events with an attention softened by pity.

Commendatore Visanio sat at the table but did not eat. He pulled his napkin from the napkin ring as if he were unsheathing a dagger, scowled at the broth yellowing in his soup plate, in which floated a few shreds of herb, mixed with little cubes of pink turnip.

"Have you no appetite, Visanio?" Signora Trigliona asked gently. Whenever the Commendatore was tormented by something, she displayed the temperament of a Sister of Mercy.

"Appetite . . . ! Appetite . . . !" the Commendatore burst out sarcastically. "How can one have any appetite, when things like this happen"

To give greater force to his words, the Commendatore threw down the spoon with which he had already armed himself in the middle of the table, and a violent flush enflamed his face, rolling up like a spring-loaded window shade to the summit of his baldness.

"This cannot go on! I will not be made a laughing-stock by anyone, least of all by that . . . that . . ."

While Commendatore Visanio searched for the right word, Nivasio, who knew very well for whom it was intended, suffered agonies.

"Swine!" the Commendatore finally decided, and Nivasio thought he would die.

"But if you will have nothing more to do with him," Signora Trigliona replied, "then who can we turn to?"

"Who . . . ? Who . . . ? We shall see who! As if he were the only one in the world!"

"But I don't see, Visanio. . . ."

"You don't see! You don't see! Just like a woman! That's what they all say! Try writing to the Generaless, your 'great friend,' Papatrapatakos's wife. Write and ask her about that girl you say she has mentioned so many times to you. You said yourself you would only need to ask. . . . We'll see about that! If it's all roses. . . ."

Signora Trigliona was hit with her own weapon.

"You're right, Visanio," she said. And with the tip of her spoon she began to fish shreds of herb from the yellow liquid.

The response of Generaless Papatrapatakos was not slow in coming. Needless to say it was written in French:

> *Chère amie,*
>
> The girl I mentioned to you is named Pertilina. She is an orphan. On the prayers of her aunt, that saintly woman, I have placed her with the good sisters who taught my little Pipizza.[18] I recommend her with all my heart, *ma chère.* She will come straight from the convent to your house, and I am certain . . .

The paper bore the heading of General Headquarters. The next morning, standing at the window under a blazing sun, rubbing Lubin water into his beard, Commendatore Visanio sang:

> That pig will see, that pig will see
> I don't give a da-a-amn about him!

And while Nivasio silently suffered hearing his father call a demiurge a pig, the wind of happiness came gusting through Casa Dolcemare.

That same evening, at the Demotic, which is to say Municipal Theater, Eleonora Duse recited *La Dame aux camélias.* Commendatore Visanio and Signora Trigliona had front row seats for the performance. A perfect occasion for showing off the black pearl, letting it hang from its platinum chain in the shadowy triangle between breast and breast. But how wear against one's skin a jewel that had passed all the way through Sebaste's intestines?

After lunch the next day, while Commendatore Visanio and Signora Trigliona were having coffee on the veranda, the Commendatore, his cheeks blossoming with good humor, turned the conversation to the previous night's performance.[19]

"Duse has a golden voice," he said.

"Golden," confirmed Signora Trigliona, fishing sugar from the bottom of her cup with the tip of her spoon.

"Sarah Bernhardt," Commendatore Visanio went on, "may be more brilliant, *plus pétillante,* but Duse is more profound."

"More profound," Signora Trigliona confirmed.

Commendatore Visanio stood up and strolled across the veranda, jingling the coins in his pocket. He stopped for a moment with his head bowed, then looked up full of inspiration.

"E-le-o-no-ra Du-se," he pronounced, as if he were thinking aloud. Then more softly, more slowly, more to himself, he repeated, "E-le-o-no-ra."

The already deep-rooted conviction that Pertilina had delivered them from the base vexations they had been condemned to as a result of the material furnished them by Signor Forty, allowed them, even before Pertilina actually appeared, to raise their spirits to loftier dramas, to the immanence of art and poetry.

On a sudden impulse, Commendatore Visanio

emerged from his revery over the magic name and turned abruptly on his heel.

"We shall go to hear her in *La Città Morta* as well," he exclaimed.

Signora Trigliona, who was readjusting an arrangement of dahlias in a Chinese vase, said:

"Countess Minciaki tells me that *La Città Morta* is in verse."[20]

"In verse?" Commendatore Visanio repeated. And the discussion went no further.

VI.

Pertilina entered Casa Dolcemare flanked by an aunt dressed in mattress ticking and a mute uncle. Signora Trigliona was seated in an armchair. Commendatore Visanio stood beside her, his hand resting on the back of the chair.

"The girl," said Signora Trigliona, "will live with us as one of the family."

"As one of the family," Commendatore Visanio repeated.

"We will look after her as if she were our own daughter."

"Our own daughter," the Commendatore repeated.

"We will see that she goes to Mass on Sundays and feast days."

"Feast days."

"You are satisfied, I hope?" Signora Trigliona concluded, looking at the aunt.

"Yes, yes," the latter replied.

"And you, my good man?" Signora Trigliona repeated, looking at the uncle.

He stretched his neck, turned red as if he were about to produce an ostrich egg from his mouth, and said:

"Tio, tio!"

"Forgive him, madame," said the aunt, "my husband has a little trouble speaking."

To shield her from the promiscuity of the other servants, Signora Trigliona put Pertilina in a small room on their own floor.

"I entrust her to you," the aunt said beseechingly, and, lowering her voice, "the wee thing isn't even a woman yet."

"Not a woman?" Signora Trigliona said in alarm. Through her mind flashed the terrible image of Cosma the Leaper disguised as Hermione.

The aunt whispered behind her hand:

"She hasn't had her . . ."

"Ahem!" coughed Commendatore Visanio, running his fingers over his flowing beard. The mute, walking at a slant and bowing twistedly, kept repeating:

"Tio, tio . . . ! Tio, tio . . . ! Tio, tio . . . !

That night, in bed, Signora Trigliona said to Commendatore Visanio:

"Visanio, now that we have Pertilina with us, you must stop walking around the halls in your underwear."

Pertilina was slight as a shadow, fragrant with purity. Her lowered lashes shaded the modest blush of her cheeks. In her free time she set out little images of saints on her bedstead, she embroidered bleeding hearts and praying hands. The candor of her soul was reflected in the very gestures of the new chambermaid. Pertilina set fire to the master bed, dusted off an original pastel portraying Signora Trigliona in a ball gown, brought the Commendatore his supporter when he asked for his curling iron.

"She is the picture of innocence," said Signora Trigliona, "but a complete disaster."

"What of it?" replied Commendatore Visanio. "At least she has freed us from that pig Saranti."

"Pig!" thought Nivasio with a shudder of horror. "He who breathes life into clay, who commands the elements, who dispenses joy and sorrow—a pig? What blasphemy!"

The night light spread a puerile glimmer through the room. Commendatore Visanio's beard lay on the covers. Signora Trigliona's breasts rose and fell under the lace of her nightgown. The smell of the sleepers thickened in the air. A moan, threading its way through the darkness like a ribbon, slipped under the door and across the floor.

MOAN: "Oooh!" (*Signora Trigliona wakes up with a start.*)

SIGNORA TRIGLIONA: "Visanio, a moan!"

COMMENDATORE VISANIO (*rousing himself*): "Are you mad?"

MOAN: "Oooh!"

SIGNORA TRIGLIONA: "It's from Pertilina's room."

COMMENDATORE VISANIO: "Maybe those mushrooms made her sick." (*Placing his bare feet on the bedside rug.*) "I'll go and see."

SIGNORA TRIGLIONA (*clutching Commendatore Visanio's nightshirt*): "I'm afraid!"

COMMENDATORE VISANIO (*taking a small "bull-dog" revolver from his night table*): "Silly woman!" (*He goes to the door with a candle in his left hand and the revolver in his right.*)

SIGNORA TRIGLIONA: "Then I'm coming with you!"[21] (*She seizes a candlestick and follows her husband.*)

MOAN: "Oooh!"

Pertilina's door resisted the Commendatore's efforts.

"Open up!" he shouted.

"Oooh!" replied the Moan from the other side.

"Open up!" the Commendatore shouted again. And as no one, not even the Moan, answered his second order, the Commendatore turned sideways, took hold of his groin with both hands, leaned back, and with the catapult of his shoulder broke through the door.

A white shadow leaped over the windowsill and plunged into the night. The Commendatore ran to the window: the shadow he had glimpsed turned out to be the white window curtain, which blew out as he opened the door. But his investigation of the window did not prove fruitless. Two wooden poles stuck up above the sill. The Commendatore leaned out and saw that they were the tips of a ladder that went down from the window into the garden.

"Oooh!" said the Moan.

"Who is there?" shouted Commendatore Visanio, turning in the direction of the Moan.

"Sergeant Zizimakis, Twenty-seventh Infantry, Fourth Battalion, Second Company," replied the Moan.

"Aha!" cried the Commendatore, aiming the bulldog at the talking darkness.

"Don't shoot!" begged the Moan. "I've got enough holes in me."

"You're wounded? What happened? Where is Pertilina?"

"Slut!" hissed Sergeant Zizimakis. "She ran away with Sergeant Cosmazizis, Twenty-seventh Infantry, Fourth Battalion, First Company. I tried to take my turn early, and it was the end of me. . . ."

So saying, Sergeant Zizimakis expired.

Instantly the house was alert. Lights went on everywhere. Bare feet rushed up and down stairs. The people of the house were joined by people from neighboring houses. Pelopidas, holding his underpants up with his hands, ran for the Director of Urban Legal Services. Commendatore Visanio, the bulldog in his fist, stood guard before the scene of the crime.

The Colonel arrived at a gallop, escorted by a dozen *astifílakes*[22] with lighted torches. The splendid arrival of Public Authority was greeted from the windows by cheers and applause. The Colonel divided his *lampadaphori,* sending half of them around one side of the house and half around the other. When he called for the attack, he discovered that he was alone. It was a great disappointment. At that moment a voice shouted from a balcony:

"Viva Colonel Tsé!"

"Vivaaa!" answered a hundred voices from other balconies. The Colonel saluted with his riding crop, and then, with his collar turned up over is bare, red, fighting-cock's neck, and his monocle in his eye, he entered the house of the crime.

The Director of Urban Legal Services arrived just in time. Despite the threat of the bulldog, Commendatore Visanio was about to be overwhelmed by a horde of curious neighbors who wanted to get a look at the dead man. The Colonel confronted the mob.

"Stand back! Stand back! Make way for authoghity!"

Thanks to the information furnished by Sergeant Zizimakis before his death, Colonel Tsé's *astifílakes* quickly rounded up Sergeant Cosmazizis and the girl Pertilina. The pair had taken lodgings under the false name of Mazizikos and wife at the Xenodochion tou Dipylou near the Keramikos. The arrest of the murderer and his accomplice quieted public opinion, which was justifiably distressed by the crime in Casa Dolcemare.

The investigation revealed that in the little second-floor room, where Signora Trigliona had put Pertilina to spare her the promiscuity of the other servants, she had received one by one the entire Twenty-seventh Infantry Regiment, which was quartered in the Turcophagos Barracks, a short distance from the Dolcemare residence. The turns were arranged with scrupulous precision, as was revealed by a pocket calender found under Pertilina's mattress, in which, with a large, childish hand, she had entered the names of her visitors and the date assigned to each. Thus it became known that April 12th, the date of the crime, was assigned to Sergeant Cosmazizis, while Sergeant Zizimakis was assigned April 13th. This discovery cast a bright light on Sergeant Zizimakis's mysterious last words: "I tried to take my turn early, and it was the end of me." Colonel Tsé had found the tip of the thread. The rapid conclusion of the investigation constituted a personal triumph for the Director of Urban Legal Services. A few days later, Colonel Tsé was promoted to general.

From the model Averoff Prison, Pertilina wrote to Signora Trigliona asking her to send the rest of her pay, which for reasons of force majeure she was unable to come and collect in person. Signora Trigliona left the letter unanswered, which led to a new series of calamities.

A few days later, the aunt dressed in mattress ticking presented herself at Casa Dolcemare. Turned away by Pelopidas, she planted herself in the middle of the street and proclaimed at the top of her lungs that Signora Trigliona was a first-class whore, and that Commendatore Visanio had horns a mile long and everyone in the city knew it.

The sky thundered, the clouds spilled their cataracts on the scandalous voice, a diluvial rain fell on the city for seven days and nights. Patissia Avenue turned into a river. The *astifílakes* went around in rowboats. The current carried off household goods and the swollen corpses of animals. The nights were pierced by shots signaling for help, torn by the howling of dogs that had taken refuge on the roofs.

On the morning of the eighth day, the rain stopped. The low sky was mirrored in the grey water that hissed by, foaming at the corners of houses, from which the black branches of trees raised desperate invocations.

The greater part of that day, on which hope once again was able to take wing, passed without incident. Late afternoon came. Commendatore Visanio, Nivasio, Pelopidas, the women, set out on a raft to find fresh provisions. Long purple gashes on the horizon were reflected in the liquid planes. Alone in the house, languid with melancholy, Signora Trigliona sang at the piano:

> I long to die when the sun goes down . . .

The sobs of her voice, the broken chords of the piano, fell like dying butterflies among the pillows in the drawing room, when suddenly, just as Signora Trigliona was coming to the verse:

> But with the fall of evening's shade,
> I of death become afraid,

the doorbell rang violently. Signora Trigliona went to see who was there and found herself face to face with the mute.

"What do you want?" asked Signora Trigliona, trying at the same time to push the door shut again. But the mute gave a shove, came in, and slammed the door behind him.

Signora Trigliona backed away. She was red with anger and fear. Her breast heaved under the flared neck of her dressing gown.

"If you don't go away, I will call someone!" cried Signora Trigliona in a flash of inspiration, but her pretense did not have the desired effect. The mute advanced three steps, cocked his head, which was as big and yellow as a pumpkin, stood looking at the pigeon with dog's eyes, protruded his lips, and said softly:

"Tio, tio . . ."

"What do you want?" Signora Trigliona repeated.

The mute gave a start. The question distracted him from far-off thoughts. Who knows? Perhaps some obscure recollection, the suggestive glow of twilight, the song by Tosti, even love itself, that magic power which purifies the most abject creatures, was lifting his deformed soul toward the good, when Signora Trigliona's explicit demand cast him down again into the squalor of his own reality.

The gentle dog's eyes were extinguished; a pair of sharp pig's eyes flashed at Signora Trigliona.

"What do you want?"

The mute snapped his index finger against his thumb to show that he wanted money, and in a disarticulate voice said:

"Maun!"

"What?"

"Maun! Maun!" the mute repeated, his neck stretched, his veins swollen, his eyes popping out of their sockets.

Signora Trigliona's hand closed on a metal paperweight.

"If you come any closer . . ."

"Maun!" he repeated and took another step forward.

The paperweight flew over the mute's head and struck the hall mirror, opening a black star in the middle of its light.

At the back of the hall was a flight of stairs leading up to the bedrooms. In front of the stairs, the hall was traversed by a wooden railing in the middle of which was a gate armed with a cowbell. The usefulness of this railing of Helvetic style, which hitherto had eluded the keenest investigators, revealed itself brilliantly during the dramatic episode between Pertilina's presumed uncle and Signora Trigliona. But this usefulness had been foreseen neither by Commendatore Visanio nor by the designer of the railing.

The crash of the mirror falling in pieces on the stone floor covered the sound of the cowbell. In the same moment, the gate had opened and closed behind Signora Trigliona. And when, having meanwhile rushed to the floor above to take the bulldog from Commendatore Visanio's night table, she returned to the landing that divided the stairway into two branches, the mute was still madly fumbling at the gate with hands as big as sides of beef and as clumsy as feet.

"Don't move or I'll shoot!" ordered Signora Trigliona, aiming at the imbecile the six chambers of the snub-nosed pistol. Signora Trigliona put so much force into her threat that her metallic voice echoed from the four corners of the hall.

The mute rested his meaty spatulas on the railing, stretched his lips over his enormous, hooked teeth, and twisted his mouth into an immobile, soundless laugh.

The situation became static. The mute kept repeating the word "Maun," but this vocable, having lost even the sonority of an incomprehensible term, became as formless as an animal's cry.

The pink glow of twilight gradually died out. Night enveloped the man at the railing. His cry continued to sound regularly from the shadows: "Maun . . . ! Maun . . . !"

The gathering darkness increased Signora Trigliona's terror. But any attempt to open the gate would have set the Swiss bell ringing. This thought gave the besieged woman some reassurance.

"Maun . . . ! Maun . . . !"

Signora Trigliona now waited for, longed for this sinister cry. Woe if it had stopped, or even delayed.

Suddenly a feeble light came through the drawing room doorway. The streetlights had been lit. But it was not enough light to reveal the mute's movements.

Water could be heard breaking around the house. Voices passed by, a crying baby.

The big pendulum clock in the dining room rang the hours, the half hours. Seven . . . eight . . . nine . . .

In the darkness, the incarnate voice of the mute, the voice of a cunning dog, repeated:

"Maun . . . ! Maun . . . !"

At the stroke of midnight, Commendatore Visanio and Pelopidas, torn and exhausted, had only just managed to overpower the epileptic, and stood looking down at his slavering mouth, at his body lying on the floor, closed in a stony sleep.

Signora Trigliona came to in the connubial bed. Commendatore Visanio held her head up and gave her some water with a sedative. Signora Trigliona murmured:

"It's all so awful. . . . The hall mirror is broken. . . . I'm afraid. . . . Tomorrow we must have them come and bless the house."

In these sinister and inexplicable events, Nivasio recognized the vengeful hand of Signor Forty. But he did not confide his discovery to anyone.

The next day, Dom Brindisi came to bless Casa Dolcemare. He sprinkled the bedrooms, Nivasio's school room ("so that you will study more"), the other parts of the house. Before leaving, he stopped with Commendatore Visanio and Signora Trigliona for a sip of port.

"I feel better now," Signora Trigliona said to Commendatore Visanio as they came back from accompanying the priest to the door. But Commendatore Visanio, who in the bottom of his soul harbored positivist ideas, drew a few concentric circles on the lid of a hat box, took the bulldog from his night table, and went to the garden for some target practice.

At the first shot, the bulldog made a little "poof." At the second, it went "poof" again. And so with the next four shots, that is, until all the chambers were empty, this weapon which had such a deadly look, and to which Commendatore Visanio had entrusted his personal safety and that of his entire family, went poof, poof, poof, poof.

VII.

Despite its immense drink, an immense thirst returned to the earth. Nivasio saw the throat of our mother gape open, he felt the breath of her most abysmal viscera fanning his face. The voices of the Deep whispered in his ear, the Mystery of Sex spoke to him.

Woman was the Unknown: Woman and her Obscure Wound. Something impossible to conceive even in the most summary fashion. Nivasio had tried many times to discover the mystery of this Wound, from hiding, through the keyhole, but always in vain. And even though he was a man himself, Man was also the Unknown for Nivasio, so unsure was he of himself, so doubtful of his own reality.

A precocious summer sent the citizens out earlier than usual in search of relief. Shady Kefissia, smelling of resin, was crowded with festive bands.

The train to Kefissia passed right through the city, down the middle of the street, between houses from which friends leaning out of windows waved, exchanged greetings, arranged visits with friends leaning out of train compartments.

The engine with its funnel-shaped smokestack, preceded by an enormous cow-catcher, "made" its way at a walking pace through the populace, ringing its bell all the while, like the Iron Horse of the American pioneers. The station was in the middle of a public square.

One day, in the early and sultry afternoon, Commendatore Visanio, Signora Trigliona, and Nivasio got to the square just as the train was pulling out: curtains fluttering at the windows along with handkerchiefs, smoke puffing from the smokestack, steam spurting from its sides, the connecting rods beginning to grind around.

As the train filed past the embarrassed faces of the three, a cry came from across the square: "Stop! Stop!"

A red-faced little man, panting for breath, a basket clutched under each arm, ran in vain hopes of catching up with the train.

Nivasio did not see but only glimpsed: the little man's trousers were unbuttoned, something shapeless bobbed between his legs. And of all the grotesque and frightful things Nivasio has seen in his life, never has he seen anything so ugly, so sad, so "mortal," as this unconscious man running after the Unattainable, as this bouncing sex, thrust into public view, into the light of the sun.

Having failed in their attempt to throw off the yoke of Signor Forty, Commendatore Visanio and Signora Trigliona were forced to capitulate to the invincible authority of the agent. Nivasio's soul was radiant.

Signor Forty was too self-assured to harbor any resentment, and when the two penitents appeared before him covered in shame, he gave no sign that he was aware of that which in the consciences of the guilty ones themselves had the clear character of a betrayal.

To seal the happy resumption of relations, Signor Forty sent that same day to Casa Dolcemare a "pearl" fresh from the islands: Cleopatra.

Cleopatra's face was as closed as a strongbox. Nothing foretold that in a few days the ice between the new hired girl and the master's son would be broken.

That morning Nivasio was alone in the house. It was May. The donkey of the greengrocer who brought vegetables to the houses brayed heartrendingly under Casa Dolcemare's drawing room windows, where Nivasio, seated at the polished Kaps, listlessly practiced the most difficult passages from the *Konzertstück* of Carl Maria von Weber. But the already summery languor in the air, the sense of temporary independence granted by the absence of his parents, the thought that this independence ought to be made use of without delay, opposed themselves to the prolonging of this pianistic labor.

Nivasio got up from the Kaps with such an abrupt turn that the stool spun around a few more times on its threads.

Impatience and indolence vied with each other in Nivasio's heart, a thousand desires merged in him. There were so many things that could be done in his parents' absence that Nivasio did not know where to begin and finally did none of them.

He wandered from room to room. In the pantry under the stairs, he stopped to look through the wire mesh at an apricot tart covered with fly-netting. On the wood of the tempting cupboard he reread the words he himself had written there some time earlier: "The Torture of Tantalus."

He went back to the dining room. By means of a well-tried system of pulling out a drawer and sliding the bolt from inside, he opened the doors of the credenza and took from the bottom shelf a bottle of cognac and the box of Havana cigars.

This box was a gift from Etem Pasha, commander-in-chief of the Ottoman army, to Commendatore Visanio. And he, a great smoker of cigarettes but an avowed enemy of cigars, had put the fragrant box in the bottom of the credenza and thought no more about it.

The notion of profiting from the Pasha's gift occurred to Nivasio every time an occasion presented itself for getting into the credenza.

Though these occasions were rare, the first layer of Havanas was already used up, and there were beginning to be gaps in the second.

The cognac was a very fine three-star Martel, which Commendatore Visanio used to buy on the Marseilles mail boat. Nivasio tossed off two shots of it, then stretched out in Commendatore Visanio's armchair and lighted a cigar, rolling it slowly in the flame of the match.

Three boxes of matches lay on the table next to the armchair, beside Commendatore Visanio's favorite ashtray.

At that time, and thanks chiefly to Italy, the match industry had reached a high level of civility. Apart from its usefulness, the box of matches was an object which spoke to the eyes and the mind. Commendatore Visanio, like everyone else in the world, was an avid collector of match boxes. Of the three that lay within Nivasio's reach, one pictured a hunter urging on his dog: "Go, Fido, fetch the partridge!" The second showed a noble youth offering flowers to a maiden:

> The holidays are just a month away,
> And yet my lady looks so cross today!

On the third, under an old man sitting dejectedly in front of an empty keg, was written: "The Keg of Lorenzo."

Nivasio had already smoked several cigars in his life, but he had not yet managed to overcome the dizziness and nausea caused by his first cigar.

After a few puffs, Nivasio threw the Havana out the window and sat motionless in the armchair, his head resting on the back and his eyes closed.

Cigars were for Nivasio what a pipeful of opium is for others: a prelude to a state of visionary intoxication.

The intoxication began. Behind the curtain of his eyelids, Nivasio plunged into the void in a series of leaps. He thought intensely of the upstairs bathroom (the servants' bathroom was in the cellar, but unapproachable) as the only place which could afford him comfort and security in his crisis.

He staggered to his feet, left the dining room, and began to climb the stairs, grasping the banister with both hands.

In the upstairs hall, the darkness was broken by the bright rectangle of an open door. Signora Trigliona's room was full of sunlight. It was animated by a fresh splashing and the harsh murmur of a scrub brush on the floor.

Not out of curiosity, but only to find a support from which to propel himself down the hall, Nivasio leaned against the door post. The furniture was pushed back to the walls, and in the cleared center of the room, Cleopatra, scantily dressed, a brush slipped onto her bare foot, was washing the floor with soap and water.

Nivasio glimpsed the disorder in his mother's room. That the sight was real, if unexpected, did not occur to him. He blamed it on the "cursed cigar," and, helped by the archipelagoes of soap suds that were spread across the room, collapsed on the floor, while the naked foot of Cleopatra, which until then had shone like a phosphorescent foot, suddenly went out.

When Nivasio came back to his senses, his body was lying on the ground, his head resting on Cleopatra's knee, his face very close to the bare, wet feet of the island girl, which because of the short distance seemed huge, inhuman, monstrous.

The passage from a state of unconsciousness to one of consciousness went almost unnoticed. Though awake, Nivasio was hypnotized by those two bare feet, which loomed before him like mountains.

The sun irradiated the room. Invisible elements of the air penetrated Nivasio's organism.

A fly came to rest on Cleopatra's foot. Her toes jumped up together like five little people: papa, mama, and three children arranged according to height.

It was not the comicality of the movement (exceptional physiological conditions prevented Nivasio at that moment from appreciating any form of comicality) but "something else," something Nivasio felt without being able to account for it, that caused him to make that involuntary and "mechanical" gesture; that gesture he had neither willed nor thought of; that gesture the results of which he had not foreseen; that gesture which he made almost despite himself, and which, when he thought it over later with a cool head, seemed to him so bold that he could not understand how he had had the courage to do it.

Nivasio reached out his hand, grasped those moving toes, and held them tightly to make them stop. But the toes, soft yet strong, went on moving, living in Nivasio's hand.

A shiver ran up his spine.

As if it had sprung from that shiver, Nivasio heard behind him the sudden, joyless laughter of the island girl.

He, too, began to laugh.

The duet was confined to touching. A dialogue between the hand of Nivasio and the foot of Cleopatra. A dialogue between ten digits: five of them quick and nervous, the other five soft and clumsy as a newborn child. Struggling, clutching, intertwining. And this dialogue was great in its developments, infinite in its variations.

They were both laughing, nervous, excited. And they never spoke, never even looked at each other.

Many years later, having read the Epistles of St. Paul, Nivasio understood that a woman's foot is a great instrument of lust, one of the most insidious weapons the Adversary can use to lead us into temptation.

The battle that the Adversary gave Nivasio Dolcemare this time was bitter indeed.

For two days in a row, Nivasio found the door of sin open.

It was the start of the season, when women began to try out their new summer clothes, and went around the streets of the city like mad hens, eyeing each other sternly, stopping with a scowl to sniff each other's behinds.

On the day after the "day of the feet," Nivasio again found himself free of parental control. Shortly after Commendatore Visanio left for his office, Signora Trigliona also went out to see her dressmaker. But before she left, she said to Cleopatra: "Please, Cleopatra, be sure not to let the young man get into any mischief." Admirable precaution!

Experience is slow in bringing home its lessons. Though Nivasio had only just drawn from Etem Pasha's cigars the results we have seen, on the next day, finding a new chance to get into the credenza, he did not hesitate a moment to light up another Havana.

Reeling with dizziness, Nivasio climbed upstairs, heading for the mirage of the bathroom. Signora Trigliona's door was ajar, and in the shaft of light Cleopatra could be seen in the middle of the room, motionless in the sunlight that framed her, standing with her head bent and her hands on her breast.

Nivasio was unable to understand what the island girl was doing, and leaned back, full of curiosity, against the opposite wall, where he could watch without being seen.

Cleopatra held her blouse open with both hands. From the gap of the material dawned a sphere of opalescent flesh tipped by a brown, sightless eye.

The visions induced by the Pasha's cigars were taking on an unusual richness.

Nivasio and Cleopatra looked at each other through the crack of the door. Timid to the point of complete paralysis, but convinced that where he stood across the hall Cleopatra could not see him, Nivasio staunchly met the island girl's glance.

That sightless eye exercised on Nivasio the invincible attraction of a snake's eye on a chicken.

Nivasio crossed the hall, pushed the door open, stepped into the light.

He moved like a sleepwalker.

The breast shone amid the lace of the blouse like a candied fruit in a perforated paper wrapper. The nipple was strawberry-colored.

The encounter came. They rolled together on Signora Trigliona's still unmade bed. That breast which had promised so much from a distance, Nivasio discovered, after a quick capture, was not only blind but also "mute." He sensed that the real discoveries lay elsewhere, and were to be reached by other means. He fought for these new discoveries, for these new means, to which Cleopatra opposed her elbows and fists, raising a wall of hard, dumb, animal resistance.

A bell rang far away. Nivasio jumped up, ran and hid in the bathroom. His heart leaped in his throat, but all his dizziness had vanished.

During these two encounters, in which the mysteries of the flesh were revealed to Nivasio, he and Cleopatra never exchanged a word, never so much as looked at each other. Further occasions for continuing these arousing and inconclusive games did not present themselves.

Days passed. One afternoon, Nivasio and Cleopatra met between the kitchen and the ironing room. Cleopatra, without looking at Nivasio, without even stopping, whispered to him in the profound and bitter voice of a trained animal:

"Tonight, at ten, by the garden gate."

The garden of the Dolcemare residence opened onto a private lane. At night, the lane was deserted and lit by a single streetlamp, which for the sake of economy the gas company turned off at nine.

A little before ten, Nivasio crossed the garden and went out the gate. He had given no thought to why Cleopatra had made him this invitation, nor to what he might find outside the gate. He glimpsed two shadows a few steps away. Cleopatra came up to him and took his hand. The other shadow was a gunner over two meters tall, who wore spurs and a sabre that clanked like a saucepan. Up close, the gunner gave off a sour smell of cold broth and boot grease.

Nivasio found himself involved in a situation far different from what he expected.

The soldier said he was honored to make the personal acquaintance of the "young sir," about whom he had heard so many good things from Miss Tsokas.

"Miss Tsokas?"

Cleopatra's laughter flashed in the darkness.

"Miss Tsokas is me."

Nivasio felt as if he were in his mother's drawing room. They treated him with respect, like a coeval.

Without transition the gunner went on to say that he was studying French.

"Of course you must know French very well?"

"Yes," said Nivasio in a wispy voice.

The giant raised his enormous hand to point to the sky, and spread his square fingers like a fan.

"*Le ciel,*" he exclaimed in the voice of a deaf mute, "*le firmament.*"

From the shelter of the darkness, which made it impossible to follow the direction of his eyes, Nivasio studied this Ajax in jackboots, thinking that Cleopatra would not refuse such a man what, in their wrestling on Signora Trigliona's bed, she had so stubbornly refused him.

He thought, besides, "If Cleopatra *has* this soldier, why did she play those games with me for two mornings in a row?"

In his question there was not the least trace of jealousy. Nivasio heard Cleopatra talking and laughing in the dark, behaving like any other woman, and did not even think of connecting this "nocturnal" Cleopatra with the "matutinal" Cleopatra, the mute Cleopatra, the Cleopatra of the "games."

The gunner waved his hand like a rug-beater, repeating in his deaf-mute's voice:

"Dieu . . . l'infini!"

While Nivasio was trying to penetrate the mystery of this dualism, the soldier signaled for silence. Then he sang:

La Vierge inconsolable
Qui calme mon amour,
Au ciel au ciel au ciel
J'irai la voir un jour.

Nothing else happened that night.

For the rest of the time that Cleopatra remained in service at Casa Dolcemare, the relations between her and Nivasio were cool, distant, not only as if there had never been anything between them, but *as if they had quarreled.*

One day Cleopatra left. She left on good terms. The fact was so unusual that it is worth recording. She married the gunner over two meters tall and went to live with him. A strange coincidence: this same gunner, meanwhile promoted to sergeant, on a clear spring morning, followed the coffin of Commendatore Visanio, his sabre at his side, carrying the cushion of black velvet on which lay the cross of the Order of the Savior, while the military band walked behind, playing the Funeral March "for a dead hero" from Beethoven's Sonata, Opus 26.

At Cleopatra's wedding, Nivasio received a little gauze bag full of candy. He did not eat the candy. It remained intact like candy made of marble, like artificial candy, like candy to be placed in a tomb for the personal use of the dead. And what strange feelings came over him when he remembered how he had once "played" with this married woman's breasts!

Boredom began to spread like an enormous stain over Nivasio Dolcemare's life. And slowly, irresistibly, Nivasio Dolcemare sank into the quicksand of Voracious Boredom, of Thirsty Boredom, of Boredom that sucks in both body and soul.

Life had paled to a uniform, opaque whiteness. All activity that might be called not even happy but merely pleasant ceased. It seemed than an epidemic of "nullity" had silently swept over the world. Apart from such indispensible quotidian acts as sitting down to meals twice a day, and those few "duties" forced on him by the will of others, Nivasio was reduced to a total, dull, dense apathy, which diminished his faculties, clouded his eyes, filled his head with a drowsy buzz.

The sultriness of the day stifled every movement, every sound. The house was dark as a crypt, silent as a tomb. Sleep ruled over it for long hours. Nivasio, who felt no need for himself to share in the common sleep, the "familial" sleep, because he was entirely enclosed in his own private sleep, was forced during those "dead" hours to go around on tip-toe, to avoid passing near the bedrooms, to behave like a custodian of the deceased.

These "closed" hours, when the air in the house was as thick as gelatine, and a great prohibition, a stern impossibility, an immoveable, categorical "no" weighed on the house from attic to cellar, Nivasio spent illegally at the little window of a store-room full of piled-up trunks, unused furniture, stacks of old illustrated magazines, which was the most secluded place in the house, furthest from the command posts, the vital nerve centers.

Nivasio climbed up to the window and looked out at the creamy, seething heat. The sky was made of white sheet-metal. The solitary, tragic song of the last serving girl to finish washing the dishes died away nearby, and the drawn-out chirr of the cicadas was left naked.

He began dreaming in the light. "Pastirel," "Iolscom," "Momoroderiano," unknown, improbable names, but which certainly existed and belonged to people in this or some other life; the names, perhaps, of his best, of his only friends, came and went through Nivasio's head. And behind the names passed things, facts that existed beyond truth: machines, cities, entire countries, a different, unaccustomed world revealed itself to Nivasio's dazzled eyes.

To the right of the garden lay a field surrounded by a rustic wall, on which hung a sign announcing: "Field for sale." Beyond the wall lay the railroad tracks.

While he was "dreaming in the light," Nivasio looked at things confined to their short, violet shadows, but without seeing them. This time, too, he looked for a long while at some "thing" without seeing it; and even when he did see it, he continued to look at it for a long while without comprehension.

The wall that surrounded the field had fallen down in one place. The stones sprawled on the ground had left a small breach, beyond which lay black piles of excrement with flies buzzing around them.

A wagon filled with stones stood in front of the opening. The horse, inert and as if dead on its feet, touched the ground with its muzzle; its dejected ears stuck up through a ridiculous straw hat. Behind the wall, in the narrow shade, something was moving . . . a man . . . the carter.

Nivasio did not immediately understand. That straining mouth, that devilish look. . . . The man noticed Nivasio at the window and made a sign with his free hand. . . .

Nivasio threw himself back and fell to the floor of the store-room. He could not see, or hear, or think. The full horror of humanity was revealed to him in a flash. He understood why Lucifer was cast out of Heaven, why Man is condemned to die, why stench and decay are the natural end of life.

Darkness slowly fell over the trunks, the unused furniture. Nivasio heard someone calling him repeatedly and insistently. A star shone in the rectangle of the window.

But if life would not grant him a pure look, a lofty voice; if life would speak only of squalor and death, why answer that call, why return to the house?

HERE ENDS THE CHILDHOOD
OF
NIVASIO DOLCEMARE

Notes

(Translator's additions are enclosed in square brackets.)

[1]"Feminine" men cultivate an excessive love for their own mothers, love to speak of this love, to exalt it, exhaust in their love for their mothers any possibility of loving other women. What to think, on the other hand, of a man like St. Ambrose, who in his literary work, vast as it is, never once mentions his mother?

[2]Called "ireos" in the manner of the time.

[3]"Camphor" was Countess Minciaki, "Belladonna" Doctor Balano, who had set Nivasio's arm in plaster a year before following a fracture; "spit on hot iron" was Calliope, the blank young seamstress who came to work at Casa Dolcemare during the day.

Tum porro varios rerum sentimus odores,
Nec tamen ad nares venientes cernimus umquam.

For Lucretius, the odor of the human body came from invisible particles that the body gives off around itself. Lucretius's opinion could form the basis of a theory of physical odors in relation to individual character. The more passionate a man is, the more filth he produces. (An axiom to be taken metaphorically as well.) The passions are fire and movement, causing a greater organic activity, a more rapid renewal of cells, a more abundant flow of suppurative matter: a greater amount of filth. A very strict connection could be established between a man's temperament and the quality of his skin. Beware, brothers, of odorless men, but trust a greasy skin. A dry, closed skin denotes hypocrisy, egoism, frigidity. We know men whose skin gives the impression of ivory: ossified men, however young they may be. Their skin is "naturally" clean, that is, unproductive, though they may wash less often than Wolfgang Goethe.

When Calliope, the young *raftra* (seamstress), provided him with a new sailor suit, and tried it on him with her cold fingers to see if the underarms needed "letting out" or if the "crotch" was too tight, Nivasio closed his eyes, and behind the shelter of his eyelids suffered infernal torments.

[4]Filthy, in German.

[5]*Abito talare* [in Italian]: an ankle-length costume; *talare* from the Latin *talus,* ankle, whence the Italian *tallone,* heel, and *Talari,* winged shoes.

[6] *Nisus ait: "Dine hunc ardorem mentibus addunt*
Euryale? an sua cuique deus fit dira cupido?"

(Publii Virgilii Maronis, *Aeneis,* libro IX.) Thus Torquato Tasso:

> *. . . o Dio l'inspira*
> *O l'uom del suo voler suo Dio si face.*
>
> [. . . either God inspires him
> Or man makes a God of his own will.]

[7]"did not live . . . the life:" the internal accusative, similar to the Latin *coenare coenam* or *pugnare pugnam.*

[8] *Ma poi, come da gridi astretto e vinto,*
Di conserto *con lui ruppe il silenzio.*

[But then, as if maddened and overcome by cries, *In concert* with him he broke the silence.]

(The *Aeneid* of Virgil, translated [into Italian] by Annibal Caro, Book II, 219.)

[9]*dolcissima* [in Italian]. While searching for the right qualifier for the compassion inspired in him by the Greek God, Nivasio Dolcemare created his first pun, that respectable if not much-respected form of wit. *Compassione dolceamara* [lit. "bittersweet compassion"] is what came to him. The pun was spontaneous, not calculated. It struck Nivasio as a revelation. Until then, Nivasio Dolcemare had never considered the meaning of his own name, the mechanism, the punning possibilities of his name. His name was mute for him, anonymous, closed, so that Dolcemare could as well have been Dolcamara or Melcadoro. The

unforeseen pun gave him an impression of light, of a door being opened, of a new horizon. This first pun constituted an "historic turning point" in Nivasio Dolcemare's life, like the discovery of America in the life of the world. Which is not surprising. The pun has a sacred character. Besides which, the pun is the most direct, the liveliest, the most ingenious form of etymology. It is a sudden light projected from "within," from the "mechanism," from the "mystery" of things. It is the unsuspected but highly skillful adversary of religions. Because while religions put a gilded lid on things, the pun is a "sweeper of altars." Hence the discredit that surrounds puns, the suspicion that puns arouse in women and in all creatures who "rely" on religion.

[10]Happy wandering.

[11]For a fuller documentation of our thoughts concerning the relations between men and sleep, cf. our essay *"Delle cose notturne"* ["On Things of the Night"] (*La Ronda,* May 1920). By way of coincidence (but what a strange coincidence, which confirms the hostility and the braking-function exercised as much by sleep as by women on the bold ambitions of man!), we note that in the Iranian religion (Avesta), the Devi (demon) of sleep is a female demon. "Each day, at the first light, he (Fire, the good spirit, the main symbol of Ahura Mazda and the personification of petroleum: from the flames of burning naphtha that lit up the nights on the Caspian peninsula of Apscheron, where Zarathustra received his revelations) rouses the domestic rooster because his cry drives from the eylids of the living the female demon of sleep, called Busyasta of the Long Hands (she has long hands because she uses

them to close and obstruct the eyes of mortals); then, in a loud voice, he asks the head of the household for a good supply of dry wood" (Zarathustra, *Avesta,* translated [into Italian] with an historical introduction by Italo Pizzi, Istituto Editoriale Italiano, Milan).

[12]The servant goods furnished by Signor Forty were imported from the Greek archipelago, because island women have the reputation of being particularly good at household tasks: from Naxos rich in grapes, from Dònisa and Olearo in the Sporades, from Paros famous for its white marble, from Ortygia, the ancient Delos, the *floating* island of Diana and Apollo, where Zeus turned Leto into an *ortüx,* i.e. a quail.

[13]The "Chorus of the Groomi" is not sung but simply chanted to the rhythm of "Happy Gymnasts."

[14]*gameádes:* masculine substantive of the third declension *(gameàs, gameádos)* derived from the contracted verb *gaméo-gamô:* to conjugate. The meaning is not lost in the transfer, but in fact returns to its most immediate, most natural acceptation.

[15]Literally "flesh not tainted by rectal breath."

[16]It had an electric motor.

[17]This time Sebaste perfected the showing of her backside by slapping her buttocks with her hands and saying to Signora Trigliona: "Take a look in this mirror."

[18]The nubile thirty-year-old [sic] daughter of Generaless Papatrapatakos, mentioned earlier.

[19]Commendatore Visanio and Signora Trigliona went to the theater once or twice a year. In compensation, each performance left an indelible mark on them and its effects were prolonged in time. Commendatore Visanio, hearing Ermete Novelli in *Otello,* continued for years to shout every now and then in an insane voice: *"Il fazzoletto! Il fazzoletto!"* ["The handkerchief! The handkerchief!"] As for Signora Trigliona, having once heard *Madame Angot's Daughter,* she spent the rest of her life, so to speak, singing:

Et dis-donc mam'zelle Suzon
Si tu parles sur ce ton
Nom d'un nom! nom d'un nom!
Je te crêpe le chignon!

[20]*La Città Morta*—needless to say?—is not in verse. But for Countess Minciaki, for Signora Trigliona, for Commendatore Visanio; for the millions of Countess Minciakis, Signora Triglionas, and Commendatore Visanios the world over, *verse, poetry,* and *boredom* are synonymous.

[21]Man aspires to greatness, to the most specious, most magniloquent, most redundant form of greatness: heroism. When circumstances do not allow for military heroism (the most esteemed and comprehensible), man contents himself with surrogates: pioneer, explorer, builder, captain of industry. Which surrogates (even captain of industry) all imitate, inwardly and outwardly, the features of the warrior. (Symptomatic is the sympathy between military uniforms and the "fanciful militaristic costumes" of the surrogates: the semi-uniforms of bourgeois government officials during the First World War, the artful outfits in which

a Poincaré visited the front.) The epoch that spanned the nineteenth century was more pacific than warlike: but in the bosom of that pacifism, a "self-willed militarism," a "fanciful heroism" flourished more than ever, polarized in the characters of Jules Verne. Pacifism became in its turn a form of heroism. So, too, Visanio Dolcemare, an Italian and an engineer who crossed the Adriatic to bring to the plain of Thessaly the civilization of the railroad, fell into the category of the pioneers, of soldiers without armies or uniforms, of combatless combatants, of heroes without fanfares or laurels. As for the female companions of these "civilian" soldiers (Signora Trigliona, for example), they were the exact feminine counterparts of such "noble hearts of bronze." Furthermore, even though they were "army wives," the "Signora Triglionas" dressed elegantly, entertained with grace and a profound sense of fine living, loved with devotion and a dash of poetry, were dedicated to reading and dreaming, believed in the future of mankind. It is not surprising, then, that seeing her husband in danger, Signora Trigliona (although she was afraid; she herself admitted, "I'm afraid!" but only the courage of the frightened has any value) seized the candlestick and followed her husband. Because Signora Trigliona, any Signora Trigliona, was ready to follow her husband, whether it was to confront the Moan in Pertilina's room, or a fire, a flood, an earthquake, a cholera epidemic, a business failure, a horde of Boxers. And the woman of the nineteenth century, erroneously thought to be more feminine, more "pampered," more of a "Sultana" than the woman of today, so "Amazonized" herself, that the less intelligent, the less loved among them ended in a pitch of arrogance, and thus the Noras of the world were born.

We will add, in conclusion, that compared with Signora Trigliona (an Italian woman and the wife of an engineer from the end of the nineteenth century), the heroines of the movies, the gun molls of the Anglo-Saxon world, are little farts.

[22]Guardians of the *asti:* the city.

Luis the Marathonist

Three hunters met in a wooded valley, by the bank of a river. Three hunters, or one might simply say three men, because at that time all men were hunters. The first came from Thessaly, the second from Crete; the third, since he was at home, did not come from anywhere. He was called Pelops and his land Peloponnesia. Peloponnesia means "the island of Pelops," which implies the cutting of the isthmus of Corinth, which was carried out by General Türr in 1893. History is full of happy anticipations. The other two had the same name, and to distinguish between them one called himself Hercules of Crete and the other Hercules of Alcmene. It was hard to see why the three hunters should be wearing such thick hides in such hot weather, but up close you would have realized that these hides were their own skin. The three hunters sat down on a stone shaped like a sofa and began to yawn enormously. Which is not to say that they were bored, since boredom implies the possibility of a different state. The sun was "lording" in the sky, a local expression meaning that it was setting and appeared larger than at the zenith. Hercules of Crete stood up, took a stone shaped like a ball, and threw it at the red disc, which made an excellent target. Hercules of

Alcmene then picked up a stone of his own and threw it further than his predecessor. Hercules of Crete flew into a rage and was about to throw a stone at the head of his homonym and rival. Pelops intervened as master of the house, and declared that in the throwing of stones, Hercules of Alcmene was better than Hercules of Crete. The valley was called Olympia, and the three hunters, without knowing it, had founded the Olympic Games.

Man is an incurable child, and games, from war to poker, are his favorite occupation. The Olympic Games caught on so well that the years began to be counted by their periodic recurrence. Every four years an enormous crowd from all parts of Greece gathered in the valley of Olympia, by the banks of the Alpheus. They came in wagons, on mule-back, by foot. Families camped in the open. The men argued politics and played at Indian wrestling, the boys made up war games and shot at blackbirds with their pea-shooters, the women prepared *scordaglía,* a mayonnaise mixed with garlic, and *coccorezzi,* which are lamb entrails wound on skewers and roasted over a fire. The crowd swarmed in the sun and stank enormously. The Olympic Games were exquisitely racist. No one could enter the competition who was not one hundred percent Greek. Alexander asked to take part in the games and was refused. "What!" exclaimed the King of Macedonia. "My ancestors came from Argos, and you forbid me to take part in your games?" When the necessary verifications were made and the fiery ruler's claims were borne out, Alexander was admitted to the foot races, the chariot races, the wrestling, the pancration, and the other competitions which together made up the games. Meanwhile there rose up the Gymnasium, the Palaestra, the Leonidium, the Bouleuterium, the Hippodrome, and the temple dedicated to Jove. The god inside it was so big that even sitting down he touched the ceiling with his head. The statue was chryselephantine, and was lubricated night and day with a constant flow of oil to protect it from the heat. The radiator is not a new invention. The altar of the father of gods and men gave off such a stench of burnt fat as no stomach could have stood, except for those Levantine stomachs inured to the most repulsive foodstuffs. The arbiters of the games were called agonothetes, athlothetes, Hellanodics, and were chosen from among the most illustrious citizens of Elis. They went bare-legged, not yet having adopted the knee-socks and garters of football referees. Onippos, a famous wrestling champion, once saw victory slip from his grasp because in the heat of the struggle his shorts came undone. The arbiters decreed that from that day on the athletes must compete in the nude. "How lovely!" cried the women, clapping their hands with joy. But their husbands frowned, and by a unanimous decision women were banished from the games on pain of death. A victory at Olympia was for a Greek the height of glory, "greater than the honors of a triumph for a Roman," according to Cicero. To give the Olympian a proper welcome, his city would knock down a part of its wall, as was done in the hall of the Congress of Vienna so that Talleyrand could enter at the same time as the representatives of the states that defeated Napoleon, but not by the same door. Our journalists call all athletes who take part in the Olympics "Olympians," practicing a form of white magic intended to make all of our "azurri"* winners.

Even poets, historians, and orators took part in the competition, and when Herodotus read before assembled Greece his noble history of the terrible Persian Wars, the enthusiasm reached such a height that the nine books of his History were by acclamation given the names of the nine muses. The poetic competitions were revived in the modern Olympics, and in the games at Anvers, the palm of Olympian poet went to an Italian: Raniero Nicolai. Nationalist rigor was relaxed in the time of Roman Greece; in any case, it was hard to close the stadium to an emperor. Nero took part in the Olympics during his famous tour of Greece; he sang, recited, drove his chariot at a gallop behind six horses as white as unicorns, fell off at the end and disappeared in a whirl of dust. But Christianity was on the rise. Men imagine every once in a while that they have discovered the truth, and that nothing should exist outside of it. In his zeal, the emperor Theodosius prohibited the Olympics in 393, and thirty years later Theodosius II destroyed the Alei at Olympia and burned the temples. Nature completed the work of men: the Alpheus overflowed its banks and washed away the Hippodrome; earthquakes did the rest. The vale of Olympia was once again as wild and uninhabited as on that day when the two Hercules and Pelops met there, melancholy, obtuse, dressed in their skins.

Many years passed and 1892 arrived. "Let us restore the Olympic Games," Count Pierre de Coubertin said one day in the great hall of the Sorbonne, rising to his

*Italian athletes who take part in international competitions [translator's note].

feet under the fresco by Puvis de Chavannes which portrays the blessed strolling across the Elysian Fields; and he added: "In the noble contests of the stadium, the peoples will become brothers." The Count de Coubertin's idea met with favor from all who wished for the good of humanity and maintained the cult of immortal beauty. The Olympic Games were revived, and with tactful courtesy the honor of the revival went to Greece, "small today, but formerly so great." Pierre de Coubertin had seen his idea crowned with success, and died happily a few years later. His heart was taken to Olympia, and now rests under the eyes of Hermes, enclosed in his little country museum, who, with that squint peculiar to the gods, looks everywhere and nowhere. Pausanias attributed the Hermes of Olympia to Praxiteles, but more recent archeology places it among copies from the Roman period.

Athens is a magnificent city, well-suited to peripatetism. The Athenians are robust and very hairy. When it became customary to shave the beard and moustache, their faces were blue up to the eyes, the same blue as the sea that washes the shores of nearby Faliron. The ranks of these black men are sometimes broken by a monumental woman, with columnar legs, round, watery eyes, two braids the color of corn and as thick as cables falling over her shoulders. In the train of Otto of Bavaria, the first king of Greece, batches of Bavarian architects arrived in the new kingdom, who filled the city with neoclassical buildings and founded, a short distance from Athens, a town consecrated to Hercules: Heracleion. To one of the blond great-granddaughters of these builders, the poet Koulouvatos has dedicated his poem *Rinalda*.

In 1896, Athens prepared to celebrate the revival of the Olympic Games. Nivasio Dolcemare had the good fortune to be present at this memorable happening, and though at the time the years of his life could be counted on the fingers of one hand, the events still shine in his memory like a phosphorous landscape under a black velvet sky.

Athens reconstructed with great diligence its magnet-shaped stadium on the left bank of the Ilissos, but did not have time to finish the magnificent stairway of Pentelic marble, which is as white and sparkling as sugar, and on the day of the inauguration, half-marble and half-wood, the immense grandstand, set amid the vegetal softness of a small suburban forest, looked like a half-shaven face, the other half brown with an eight-day beard. Then the crowd arrived and gave the stadium the uniform appearance of a jar of caviar.

To the left of the stadium stood a strange domed edifice shaped like a gas tank. It was called the Panorama and resembled the old Augusteum. Do not ask Nivasio Dolcemare if this building was beautiful or ugly: it was a friend. It was like one of those old dogs, half-blinded by cataracts, who wander through the house like shadows and seem unable to leave your side. But they do leave, and one day the Panorama left Nivasio Dolcemare, plunging him into despair. It cost four cents to get in, and for a fifth cent you could pull your horoscope on a little card from under the goose that laid golden eggs. Then, at the end of a dark corridor, would appear an encounter between French and Prussian soldiers. Finally, by means of a wooden stairway, one reached a circular platform around which turned, in the sinister light of the Last Judgment, the siege of Paris as depicted by Neuville and Detaille. The impression that the Sistine Chapel makes on Nivasio Dolcemare today bears no comparison with the impression the Panorama made on him then.

Opposite the Panorama stood, and still stands, the statue of George Averof, the generous donor of the millions of drachmae needed for the reconstruction of the stadium. Averof, despite his Russian name, was a native of the Greek village of Metzovo, and in Alexandria of Egypt had become a millionaire two hundred times over. In gratitude, Greece gave the name of her munificent son to the cruiser she bought from Italy in 1910, which, during the Balkan War of 1912, single-handedly held the Dardanelles against the Turkish fleet, which had many powerful ships, all of them equally incapable of navigating.

On Sunday, April 5th, at eleven o'clock, the festivities began with the inauguration of the stadium. The King of Serbia came especially from Belgrade with his beautiful Queen Draga. It was one of those days of slashing rain and biting wind to which the divine climate of Athens has exclusive rights. The festival committee was presided over by Constantine the Diadochos, that is, the Successor. After the inauguration ceremony, Maestro Samara led a hundred singers and three hundred players in a hymn to the Olympic Games, under blasts of wind and rain. The result was magnificent. Spiro Samara taught Nivasio Dolcemare harmony and counterpoint, or the arts of joining and separating. Samara came from Zante, like Ugo Foscolo, and like Ugo Foscolo he spoke with a Venetian accent, which gives the impression that the speaker has no teeth.

The rhetoric of fame had not yet undergone the magnificent development it has known since, and the memorable revival of the Olympic Games was begun with the modest "clack" of a pistol shot. The opening event was the 100-meter dash, which was won by an American. It was followed by other races, also won by Americans, and by the discus-throwing, that too won by an American. From the first, the Americans began taking the lion's share in the Olympic Games.

But these contests were mere appetizers before the *pièce de résistance,* which was the Marathon. In succeeding games, the forty-kilometer race has been called a Marathon by allegory, and "running a Marathon" has entered into language with the sense of running a long and difficult race. But in the first games at Athens, the Marathon race had a direct meaning, and was supposed to be an exact reproduction of the race completed in 490 B.C. by the messenger from Miltiades, who announced to Athens that the Greeks had been victorious. A perfect reproduction of that race would have required the death of the messenger, who, as we know, having reached his goal and uttered the famous *"Nenikikamen!"* fell to the ground and died. But such historical fidelity was not demanded by the spectators who crowded the stadium, for whom it was enough that the winner be a Greek. Though the victory at Marathon was two thousand three hundred and eighty-six years old, it was still very much alive in the hearts of the Greeks. Scarcely half a century earlier, Greece had liberated herself from Ottoman servitude, and many of her provinces were still under the rule of the Padishah. Turks and Persians were confused in the minds of the Greeks. Abdul Hammid was an extension of Darius. Miltiades had fought for civilization against barbarism, to which ideal the new Miltiades would have added the struggle of the true faith in Christ against the false cult of Mahomet. The new Marathon grew among the fates as both a Persian War and a Crusade. And in fact, a year later, on the plains of Thessaly, the battle of Marathon was repeated, but not as it had been prefigured in the hopes of the Greeks.

There were seventeen entrants in the race, all from different nations; "ten and seven," as the *Italian Illustrated* said at the time. There would have been eighteen if the Milanese runner Airoldi had not been excluded from the contest.

The Milanese are tenacious people, as everything in the history of their city attests. Airoldi made the journey on foot, and on foot arrived at Marathon to enter the race; but despite this magnificent effort, he was excluded from the contest because it turned out that he had raced as a professional. At that time, the laws on amateurism were strictly observed.

There were fewer foreign spectators than was hoped. To make up for it, all of Greece arose, and, some in skirts and national costume, some dressed in black according to the funereal habit of southerners, villagers and peasants hastened from all parts of "sterea," that is, solid Greece, and from the islands, with their wives, the latter either dressed in national costume, kerchiefs on their heads and strings of gold coins on their breasts, or stuffed into European silk dresses, black and shiny as the elytra of giant crickets. Carrying eggs in big, square kerchiefs, and yogurt in little wooden tubs covered with grape leaves, and straw baskets of ricotta, which they call *mizitra,* and live chickens for dinner tied by the feet, and dragging their snotty children behind them, they invaded the city, wandered the streets from morning to night, passing under the triumphal arches, among banners, flags, and oriflammes. The landowners, who bore the title of *kyrios,* lord, were recognizable by the heavy gold chains on their waistcoats and the artfully curled hairs on their moles.

Little makeshift contests served to pass the time of waiting. Eager unknowns scrambled up a pole or played tug-of-war amid general indifference. A man in shirt-sleeves and a straw hat measured the ground after the jumps. The crowd swarmed over the stands like lava on the slopes of a volcano. This human ferment gave off fumes of stale cheese and garlic, which rose into the deep and luminous sky to form a cloud shaped like a couch, on which, brightly colored and transparent, the ancient gods sat, smiling and delighted with this beautiful revival of paganism.

News arrived from time to time on the progress of the race, at which the human lava would all bend in a single wave, as if the news had a specific weight and an invisible body, and had run skimming over the warm, fragrant magma. But which, among so many truths, was the true truth? Hearing that a Greek was at the head of the few runners still in the contest, the crowd became frightened, as if in rebellion against too great a happiness. Finally, from the direction of the Panorama, a cloud of dust rose, swelled, and set loose from its breast a little group of black, running specks. A murmur arose at the same time from the depths of the stadium, an enormous ball of noise that rolled down the stairs, and from which a single word gradually emerged, a shout, a cry: Luis!

"What does 'Luis' mean?" Nivasio Dolcemare asked Frau Linda.

Luis was the little fellow in tee-shirt and shorts who came first down the black cinder track, his knees wobbling as if he were about to fall, and much too slow for the pleasure of the crowd who were on their feet shouting with red necks sticking out of their jackets, like mad geese honking with rage.

Luis came to the end of the Stadium, in front of the platform where, along with the King of Serbia and the two Queens, sat George I, King of the Hellenes, who was cross-eyed with myopia, had long, silky moustaches, and wore the flat cap of an admiral at a rakish angle. Bending his legs still more, as if he were about to kneel in excessive homage to the *basileus,* Luis raised an arm limp as an overcooked carrot, in a gesture that could either have been a salute or a call for help. A group of nearby volunteers took it in the second sense, rushed to the poor man and lifted him up in triumph.

As the most terrible fury is that of an enraged lamb, so the wildest prodigality is that of a miser overcome with generosity. Famous for their stinginess, in this outbreak of delirium, the generosity of the Greek people knew no limit or measure. Hats and sticks flew through the air. Women pulled jingling strings of gold coins from their necks and threw them to the victor. The possessors of curly moles hurled their watches with the chains behind them like little golden comets. Smoking shoes were seen passing by. The name of Luis was on every tongue, like the *bambino dall'angue* on the Visconti coat of arms. Spiridon Luis was not a professional runner. He was twenty-four years old and was born at the foot of Mount Pentelikon. His training was "natural" training, acquired by running with jars of water from Amaroussi, which for the Athenians is what Acqua Acetosa is for the Romans, a diuretic and mildly laxative mineral water. What was Luis's secret? That in a contest with scientific runners, shod in special shoes, he had run barefoot. For a Greek peasant, shoes are a useless and harmful accessory. No tanned pigskin can match the durability and elasticity of the natural footsole. Three times, in 1912, the Greeks mounted an assault on Ioannina, stronghold of the Turkish garrison; the fourth time, the Greek general shouted to his evzones: "Take off your *zaruks!*" And no sooner were the feet of the evzones freed from their gondola slippers with chrysanthemum tufts at the tips, than Ioannina was taken. Luis became the hero of the new Greece.

But Venezelos was astir. The *cunning Cretan* was working for the annexation of Crete by Greece. He had placed himself at the head of a small troop of *palikari,* had set up his general headquarters in Akrotiri, dealt on equal terms with the admirals of the great powers, whose ships were anchored in the Bay of Suda, arranged the seditious burning of the Canea, and made life unbearable for the Turkish governor Karateodori Pasha, at whose insistence, in 1897, a year after the revival of the Olympic Games in Athens, Turkey declared war on Greece.

The campaign was very brief and cost the lives of several Garibaldians who rushed to defend little Greece against the claws of the Ottoman lion. George I entrusted the command of his army to his son, the Diadochos Constantine, who in turn named as commander-in-chief his chamberlain Sapunzakis, who knew more about dining than fighting. In a short time, on the plain of Thessaly, in the presence of the ghost of Chiron, who left in disgust with the dragging step of a funeral horse, the Greek army was routed.

They ran all the way to Athens.

Who got there first?

Luis the Marathonist.

The Turks occupied Thessaly for a year, under the command of Etem Pasha, a good-natured, diabetic general, the same who had given Commendatore Visanio the box of fine cigars with which Nivasio made his beginnings as a smoker.

The years passed. Constitution Square, in Athens, is surrounded by cafés: the Select, the Tsokas, the Splendid, the Lubié. On summer nights, the square was covered with tables, and hairy, sweating men sat at them devouring ices and drinking quantities of water. In the middle of the square, between the tables of the Select and the Lubié, marriageable girls walked back and forth in gauzy dresses, escorted by their papas and mamas, who went home after these hunting trips with their tongues hanging out and their feet on fire. On the roof of the Hotel England a sheet was set up between two poles on which wavered the figures of a film based on Jules Verne's *From the Earth to the Moon*. The travelers took off in a projectile, landed on the moon, and did battle with the Selenites, who looked like toads standing on their hind legs.

Suddenly one of the hairy men sitting in the café leaped to his feet and shouted: "Etem Pasha is coming!"

At which they all stood up as one and ran off without paying their checks.

The square was left empty, and in the silence of night the round, deep, poetic call of the owl rang out.

Pallas was watching over her city.

A few years later, when the Berlin stadium was already packed and the Olympic Games were about to begin, a man came running down the track, an old man, his face covered with a fine network of wrinkles, but with moustaches sharpened by saliva and hale eyes, a ballerina's skirt around his loins and in his hand a torch bearing the sacred flame from Olympia. He had come by train, but was pretending to arrive on foot.

It was Luis the Marathonist.

Is Luis still among us? Perhaps. And perhaps not. Perhaps he is running, always first, with the skirt on his hips and the torch in his hand, through those Elysian Fields so palely portrayed by Puvis de Chavannes in the great hall of the Sorbonne, under which Pierre de Coubertin stood and called out to the world: "Let us revive the Olympic Games, and the peoples will become brothers!"

On April 8, 1939, the following notice appeared in the newspapers: "There died today, in Amaroussi, his native village, Spiro Luis, winner of the Marathon in the first Olympic Games in 1896. He was sixty-five."

Without Women

In Thessaly, near the town of Kalambaka, stands a family of column and pilaster shaped rocks known as the Meteores, which means "fallen from the sky." Some authors say that mandrakes are born in the earth from the tears of hanged men, and Achim von Arnim adds that the same plant sometimes turns into a little man, full of pride and wickedness, but lacking the divine spark that enlightens the sons of woman. So, too, the enormous stone mandrake of the Meteores may have been born from the tears of some hanged giant, one of those beastly creatures that once roamed these parts and tried to dethrone Jove, because every age has its deicides.

At the foot of the Meteores flows the river Peneus, and a short distance away the plain of Pharsalia opens out. There, from time to time, Caesar and Pompey meet in the moonlight, airy and majestic in the phosphorescent garments of ghosts, and ask each other with grand courtesy what turn the world might have taken if Pompey had won instead of Caesar, but they can find no satisfactory answer.

Thessaly is the land of centaurs and witches. Commendatore Visanio sometimes took Nivasio with him to inspect the railroad he was building across that plain consumed with dryness and swept by clouds of grasshoppers. Nivasio rode on a little grey horse and wore a little helmet on his head. Father and son were escorted by cavalrymen who wore wet handkerchiefs on the backs of their necks and carried muskets in holsters on their saddles, for protection against the *kleftes* hiding in the caves of Mount Olympus, who came down to infest the villages on the plain, to steal sheep and to extort money from the peasants.

Kleftis means brigand, but in the childish mind of Nivasio Dolcemare the word evoked the image not of a brigand, which after all is a human image, but of witches or "Thessalian wolves," as he later learned they were called by Photis, Lucius's mistress. But a brief note is necessary. *Kleftis* literally means thief, and by extension a cunning and deceitful man. The added meaning comes from the brigand's life that was forced upon the Greek patriots to avoid the Turkish police, and *kleftis,* like thief, illustrates by allegory the "thieflike" shrewdness of these hidden fighters. If a question of date did not interpose itself, the king of *kleftes* would be Ulysses.

One day the extremely sharp rays of the sun penetrated Nivasio Dolcemare's little helmet, and he fell from his horse like a lead soldier that has lost its balance. They carried him to a nearby village; he reopened his eyes in a room as cool and dark as a cellar. At first he thought he had woken up in the middle of the night, but gradually the reflection of a brighter form, of some metallic object began to shine in the darkness. His little night was punctuated by light. It was the peculiar night of a polished, fragrant drawing room of the old days, the night of an antiquarian's shop. The floor, shining like the back of a Stradivarius, reflected the feet of the armchairs. A maid came in carrying a tray with silver and crystal, gliding silently on two pieces of felt. The drawing room was "tended," that is, sheltered from sun and heat, with a care that spoke for a profound grasp of the biological necessities of a climate in which the fury of the dog days was so fierce. With exquisite simulation, the one window that allowed a little light to enter was covered by a floor-length screen on which shone a transparent green landscape with happily sparkling brooks.

A voice beside him asked, "Would you like some *neranzaki*?"

It was a tender voice, so rich in inflections that even in such a brief phrase it managed to pass three times from low to high and back again, sketching a sonorous line of little rolling mountains. At the sound of this voice, Nivasio became aware that his head was resting on the knees of an enormous, living doll, enclosed like a priest in a black habit sealed in front by an unbroken line of black buttons, who gave off that sweet odor of roses indissolubly connected in Nivasio Dolcemare's mind with the idea of semolina pudding.

Huge and round, the doll's face smiled down at Nivasio from above, as if the moon herself had come down to him to show her affection. This tender and proper woman was Signora Perdoux, widow of a Norman engineer who had also come to Thessaly to build the railroad, and had died of malaria a year before. Signora Perdoux's hand, as small and white as a gardenia, took a teaspoon from the tray that the girl was holding, dipped it into a crystal bowl, brought up a small emerald stream, skillfully curled it around the spoon, and placed on Nivasio's lips that fragrant sweetness made from unripe oranges cooked in sugar, which they call *neranzaki*. And the *neranzaki*, the shady coolness of the drawing room, the luminous landscape on the screen, the perfumed lap of Madame Perdoux were the happily combined elements of a little paradise, in contrast to the inferno of white earth and sun that simmered outside.

An equally fabulous image has been left in Nivasio Dolcemare's memory by the Vale of Tempe, the Peneus flowing through it, with willows and plane trees bowing respectfully over its banks like courtiers as the Sun King passed by. Apollo came to the Vale of Tempe to cleanse himself after killing the serpent, and in the same setting Wolfgang Goethe placed the classical witches' sabbath that Arrigo Boito clothed in undulant sound.

From some villages, minarets rise into the sky like freshly sharpened pencils, but such perfection is rare. Most of the minarets are lopped off, and on their broken tops, like big baskets, sit the nests of storks.

A wooden knocking echoes in the sky: it is a stork flying over and clapping its beak, long and pointed like the wooden scissors they use to enlarge the fingers of gloves. Another stork waits in the nest, hump-backed, standing on one leg, like a pedantic, meditative aunt. When they migrate, storks fly in triangles, and have taught the same formation to our aviators.

Storks winter in Africa and summer in Europe. On their way back to Africa, some pass over France and others over the Balkans, and only a very few pass over Italy. Why? The ring of the Alps has been given as an explanation, but it is too "physical" an explanation. It grieves me, as an Italian, that the stork does not know my country even as a bridge, and my grief is metaphysical.

The stork is a bearer of good tidings, which he brings down from the sky, as dolphins bring them up from the sea. Storks live strictly moral lives, and it is said that an adulterous stork will be tried, condemned, and executed by a tribunal of his fellow storks.

"Stork" in Greek is *pelargòs,* and Greece was once called Pelasgia. Etymology is an untrustworthy science, but the similarity between these two words is at least curious. On the other hand, we know how often and how easily an "r" can become an "s" and vice versa. Greece was the land of the Pelasgi, but also the land of the Pelargi; and who can be sure that Pelargi and Pelasgi were not the same thing, or at least that the former were not representatives, heralds, symbols of the latter? This would explain the great respect for storks among Greeks in general, and Thessaliots in particular. The stork is their god; they have taken its name, and even hope to share in its virtue; which comes down to saying that storks are the same as themselves, but deified and free to sail through the sky with their legs dangling down and their beaks going "clack clack." Totemism is a sign of the dignity animals once enjoyed, a testimony that the earth was once a paradise.

But the memory of this paradise grows more and more dim. Nivasio Dolcemare looked up the word "swastika" in the *Enciclopedia Italiana.* The compiler says that the name of this magic symbol comes from the Sanskrit *su* (good or well) and *as* (being); he mentions the solar significance of the swastika, notes that the swastika with right-turned hooks is called a "sawastika," and is a bad luck charm for the Indians, but he passes over the more poetic interpretation of the swastika, as a representation of the stork in flight. Yet our memory of the time when animals lived with us as companions and equals contains the most encouraging idea of the future of the world, an idea that lets us glimpse, beyond the contraction of peoples into themselves, their expansion into a common brotherhood, and finally their new merging with the animals in a paradise regained.

The peaks of the Meteores are crowned with very old monasteries, inaccessible by road or other paths, to which men are hauled up in nets like fish. Women are strictly forbidden access, and since the most ancient wisdom affirms that woman is a harbinger of disorder and disturbance, the monasteries of the Meteores are one of the few spots on earth where Happiness might possibly take up residence.

So, too, around 1908, thought Guelfo Civinini, when he visited the Meteores on assignment from the *Corriere della Sera*. The *igumenos,* or father superior, invited him to spend a night in the monastery, and as sleep hovered over him with spread wings in the bare cell, Civinini thought, "What peace! What serenity! You can tell that no woman has ever set foot here!"

How Civinini spent the night is not mentioned, whether he enjoyed the tranquility afforded by the absence of women, or had to struggle against the bedbugs that infest such holy houses, which in size and methods of attack are in proportion with that land of centaurs and giants. But when Civinini woke up the next morning and found a hairpin beside his cot, he exclaimed: "Even here there have been women!"

But Civinini was wrong. That hairpin had not fallen from the blond, fragrant tresses of a woman, but from the black and greasy mane of a monk. Had Guelfo not noticed that Greek monks wear their long hair in buns on the back of their necks, shining with oil and dusted with dandruff? The owner of that hairpin might never have seen a woman.

Never have seen a woman . . .

After a space of thirty years, a notice appeared in the newspapers which confirmed this otherwise inconceivable possibility. The inhabitants of the Pinsk marshes, in Poland, were unaware that there had been a World War; they did not know what a horse was, and fled in terror when they saw one; they had never seen stairs, and brought to the foot of a stairway, they began to crawl up it on all fours. But never to have seen a woman . . . ?

The notice read: "There died today, at the age of eighty-two, in a monastery on Mount Athos, Brother Michael Tolotos, who in his entire life *had never seen a woman.* Michael Tolotos, a few days after his birth, was taken from the ruins of his house, destroyed by an earthquake, and brought to the monastery, where he remained for the rest of his life."

What notion of woman could a man have who had never seen a woman? It may be possible to conceive of a creature who is closed to the impulses and emotions aroused by the sight of a woman, and it may not be. Never to have seen a woman is perhaps the best condition for receiving the influx of the "eternal feminine." Like the highest art, the highest love is not copied from nature. That touch of the physical in Dante's love for Beatrice casts a shadow on the splendor of the ineffable emotion. And when some obstacle prevents the physical fulfillment of love, love then rises to the sublime, as in the case of Heloise and Abelard. Not to mention that Michael Tolotos had seen at least one woman, not real but painted, in his monastery on Mount Athos, even if it were only the black face of the Madonna, enclosed in the silver of the icon which they call the Panaghia, or "All-holy." And one image is enough, as the image of Our Lady of Einsiedeln was enough to remind Theophrastus Bombastus von Hohenheim, known as Paracelsus, of the face of his mother, whom he had never seen. And even if the image of woman is lacking, there is still the imagining of woman. Because woman is in us more than we are in her. And just as woman was born bodily from one of our ribs, so woman as an idea is born in the innermost folds of our mind.

Fragments

Fragment No. 1

(Nivasio Dolcemare, before falling from his horse smitten by sunstroke, rode across the plain of Thessaly at the side of his father, Commendatore Visanio.)

In the torrid valley of the Peneus, a short distance apart, Dolcemare father and son proceed on foot, each in the short shadow of his own mount. The earth is white, cracked in long X's and Z's. Of what had once been the river, a glaze of water remains in the sand, and stretches shining to the horizon like a silver road.

Fragment No. 2

(Having fallen from his horse, Nivasio Dolcemare is taken to the house of the widow Perdoux.)

The sun has set. Signora Perdoux moves Nivasio Dolcemare's chair out onto the terrace, sits down beside him, and begins to tell him stories. Between one story and the next, as if to make the necessary connection between fable and reality, Signora Perdoux, who has no children and so is all the more subtly a mother, points with her soft, white hand to the peak of Mount Olympus and says: "Do you see those mountains, my child? They are full of brigands who stop travelers and rob them, and if anyone resists, they go boom boom."

Fragment No. 3

Sunk into the armchair which is too big for him, Nivasio does not listen to the stories Signora Perdoux tells him, but only to the sound of her voice. He listens to this voice *as if from another life.* Interrupted by the brief death of sunstroke, his vital activity has not yet recovered its regular rhythm.

Nivasio sees even the form of Signora Perdoux as if from another life. The form of Signora Perdoux is monumental and at the same time extremely soft, the form of a more-than-mother, of a mother goddess, of an indirect and ineffable mother.

The relations between mother and child might be more delicate, more amiable, more poetic, if there were no blood ties between them; if each mother made herself the mother not of her own children but of some other mother's children. Then even the most difficult, the most demanding children, even children with the deepest and purest needs, would be able to savor that "poetry of the mother" which until now has been reserved for plebeians.

Signora Perdoux's physical qualities justify the fascination she exercises on Nivasio Dolcemare.

Signora Perdoux is neat, tidy, extremely well-kept. She has reached the stage of life in which the skin and the soul no longer secrete any humors. Grown old, a woman becomes a girl again, and recovers, beyond the foul storm of the passions, a candid virginity, the prelude to that supreme virginity which is death.

NB: We might have thrown these fragments away, but what better conclusion could this book, or any book, have than the notion of "death as the supreme virginity"?

The Eridanos Library

1. *Posthumous Papers of a Living Author,* by Robert Musil
2. *Hell Screen, Cogwheels, A Fool's Life,* by Ryunosuke Akutagawa
3. *Childhood of Nivasio Dolcemare,* by Alberto Savinio
4. *The Late Mattia Pascal,* by Luigi Pirandello
5. *Nights as Day, Days as Night,* by Michel Leiris
6. *The Waterfalls of Slunj,* by Heimito von Doderer

Eridanos Press, Inc., P.O. Box 211, Hygiene, CO 80533.

This book was printed in February of 1988 by
Il Poligrafico Piemontese P.PM. *in Casale Monferrato, Italy.*
The Type is Baskerville 12/13.
The paper is Corolla Book 120 grs. for the insides
and Acquerello Bianco 160 grs. for the jacket,
both manufactured by Cartiera Fedrigoni, Verona,
especially for this collection.